YEAR PLANNER

- 2019 -

- JULY -

S	M	T	W	T	F	S
	1	2	3	4	5	6
7	8	9	10	11	12	13
14	15	16	17	18	19	20
21	22	23	24	25	26	27
28	29	30	31			

- AUGUST -

S	M	T	W	T	F	S
				1	2	3
4	5	6	7	8	9	10
11	12	13	14	15	16	17
18	19	20	21	22	23	24
25	26	27	28	29	30	31

- SEPTEMBER -

S	M	T	W	T	F	S
1	2	3	4	5	6	7
8	9	10	11	12	13	14
15	16	17	18	19	20	21
22	23	24	25	26	27	28
29	30					

- OCTOBER -

S	M	T	W	T	F	S
		1	2	3	4	5
6	7	8	9	10	11	12
13	14	15	16	17	18	19
20	21	22	23	24	25	26
27	28	29	30	31		

- NOVEMBER -

S	M	T	W	T	F	S
					1	2
3	4	5	6	7	8	9
10	11	12	13	14	15	16
17	18	19	20	21	22	23
24	25	26	27	28	29	30

- DECEMBER -

S	M	T	W	T	F	S
1	2	3	4	5	6	7
8	9	10	11	12	13	14
15	16	17	18	19	20	21
22	23	24	25	26	27	28
29	30	31				

- 2019 -

First published in Great Britain in 2018 by Victor Gollancz Ltd.
A member of the Orion Publishing Group,
Carmelite House, 50 Victoria Embankment, London EC4Y 0DZ

Isobel Pearson, Reb Voyce, Bernard Pearson and Ian Mitchell
trading as Discworld Emporium

With great thanks to Rob Wilkins, creative consultant

Additional illustrations by Peter Dennis
Typeset by Amanda Cummings

ISBN 978 1 4732 2310 3

Printed in China

DISCWORLD
QUIZ DIARY
2019
'WIZARDS WERE RUMOURED TO BE WISE – IN FACT, THAT'S WHERE THE WORD CAME FROM*
*FROM THE OLD WYS-ARS. LIT.: ONE WHO, AT THE BOTTOM, IS VERY SMART'
TERRY PRATCHETT
SOUL MUSIC

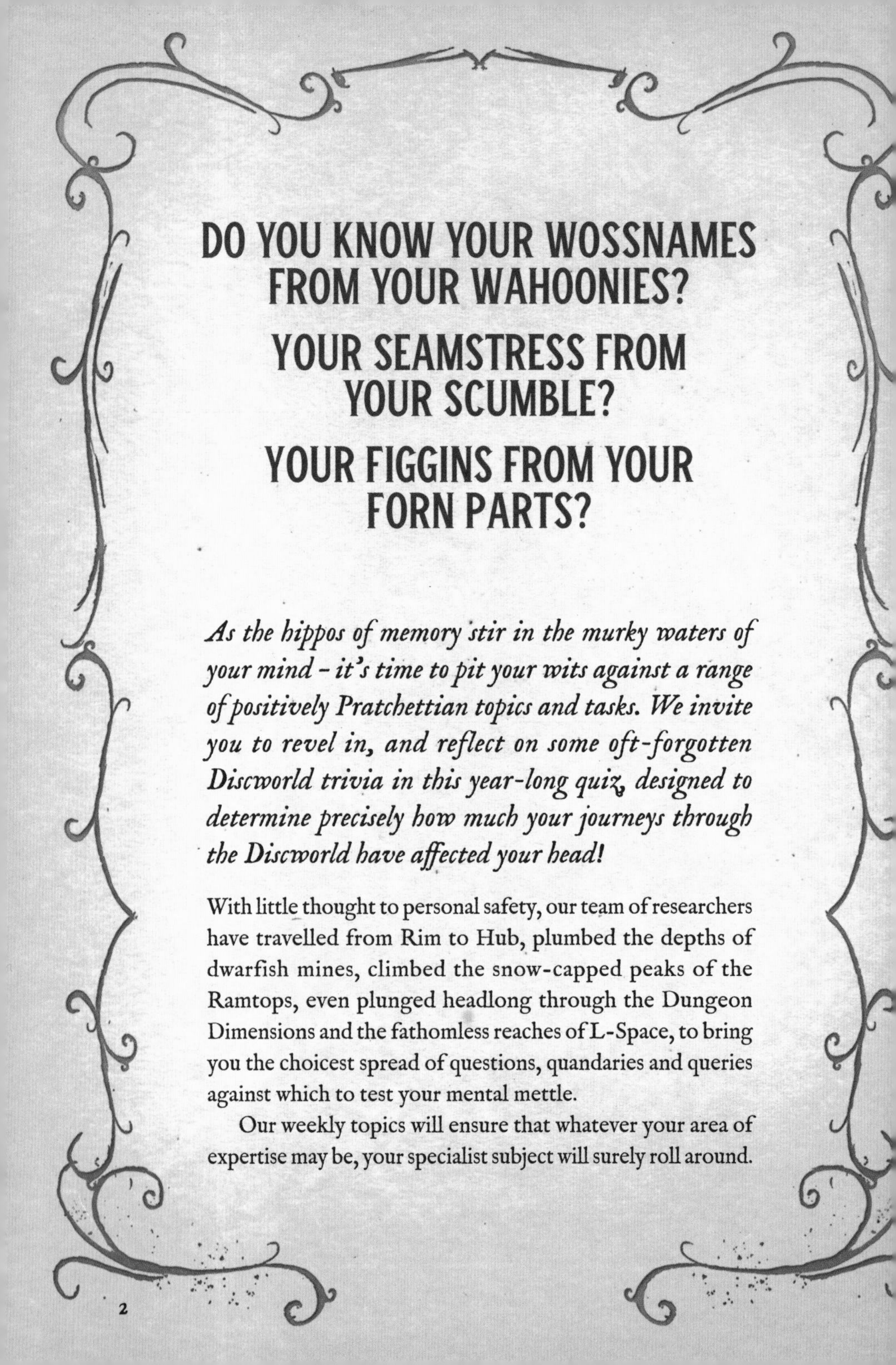

DO YOU KNOW YOUR WOSSNAMES FROM YOUR WAHOONIES?

YOUR SEAMSTRESS FROM YOUR SCUMBLE?

YOUR FIGGINS FROM YOUR FORN PARTS?

As the hippos of memory stir in the murky waters of your mind – it's time to pit your wits against a range of positively Pratchettian topics and tasks. We invite you to revel in, and reflect on some oft-forgotten Discworld trivia in this year-long quiz, designed to determine precisely how much your journeys through the Discworld have affected your head!

With little thought to personal safety, our team of researchers have travelled from Rim to Hub, plumbed the depths of dwarfish mines, climbed the snow-capped peaks of the Ramtops, even plunged headlong through the Dungeon Dimensions and the fathomless reaches of L-Space, to bring you the choicest spread of questions, quandaries and queries against which to test your mental mettle.

Our weekly topics will ensure that whatever your area of expertise may be, your specialist subject will surely roll around.

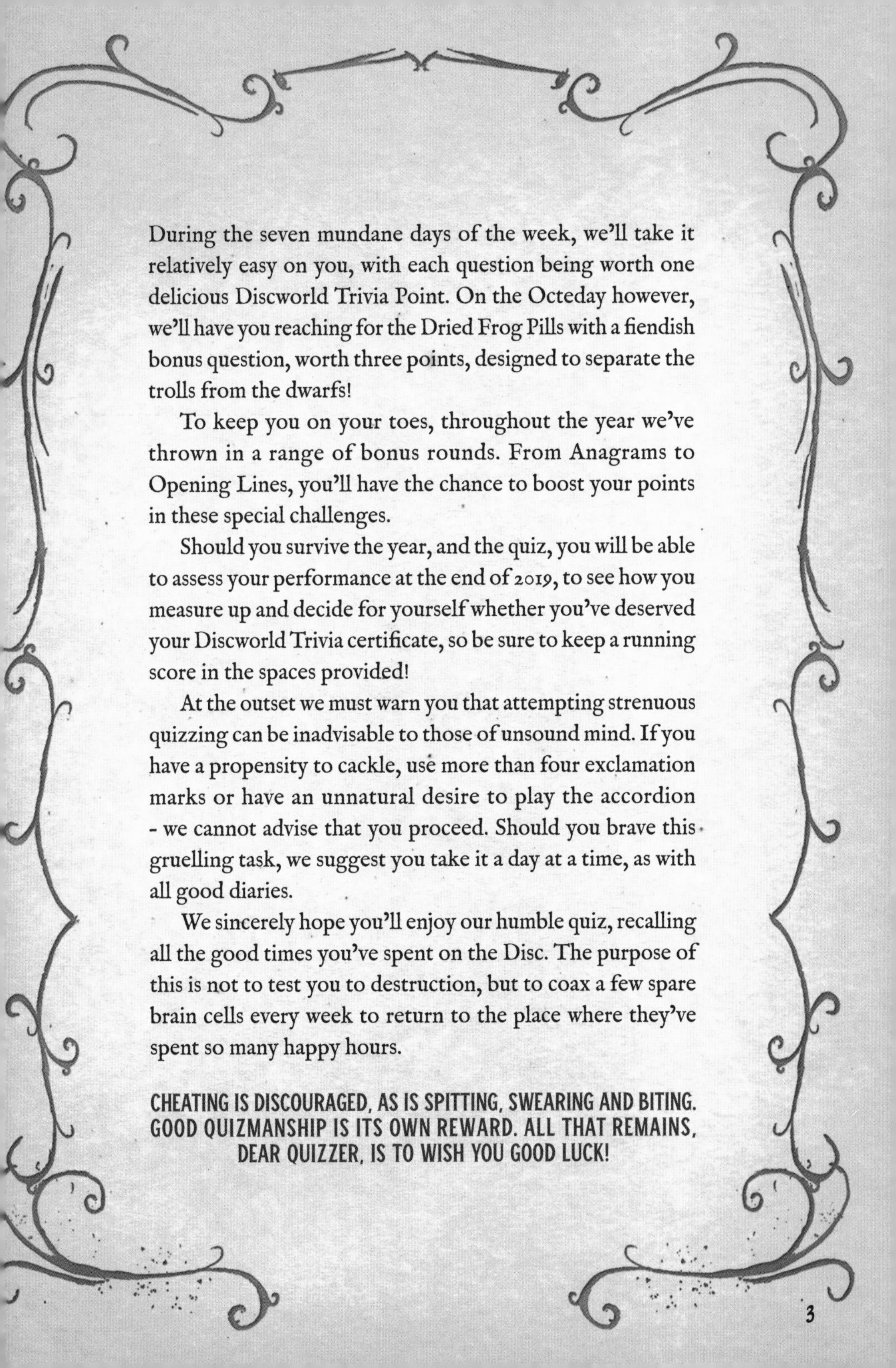

During the seven mundane days of the week, we'll take it relatively easy on you, with each question being worth one delicious Discworld Trivia Point. On the Octeday however, we'll have you reaching for the Dried Frog Pills with a fiendish bonus question, worth three points, designed to separate the trolls from the dwarfs!

To keep you on your toes, throughout the year we've thrown in a range of bonus rounds. From Anagrams to Opening Lines, you'll have the chance to boost your points in these special challenges.

Should you survive the year, and the quiz, you will be able to assess your performance at the end of 2019, to see how you measure up and decide for yourself whether you've deserved your Discworld Trivia certificate, so be sure to keep a running score in the spaces provided!

At the outset we must warn you that attempting strenuous quizzing can be inadvisable to those of unsound mind. If you have a propensity to cackle, use more than four exclamation marks or have an unnatural desire to play the accordion - we cannot advise that you proceed. Should you brave this gruelling task, we suggest you take it a day at a time, as with all good diaries.

We sincerely hope you'll enjoy our humble quiz, recalling all the good times you've spent on the Disc. The purpose of this is not to test you to destruction, but to coax a few spare brain cells every week to return to the place where they've spent so many happy hours.

CHEATING IS DISCOURAGED, AS IS SPITTING, SWEARING AND BITING. GOOD QUIZMANSHIP IS ITS OWN REWARD. ALL THAT REMAINS, DEAR QUIZZER, IS TO WISH YOU GOOD LUCK!

– JOGRAFFY! –

TUESDAY 1ST JAN

1. **What is the name of the circular sea, into which the River Ankh eventually oozes?**

☞ ______________________

New Year – Public Holiday UK
Hogswatch Day

WEDNESDAY 2ND JAN

THURSDAY 3RD JAN

2. **By which name is the ten mile high mountain at the center of the Disc known?**

☞ ______________________

ANSWERS

1. *The Circle Sea*
2. *Cori Celeste*
3. *The Wyrmberg*
4. *Jerakeen (The Fifth Elephant's name remains a mystery!)*

FRIDAY 4TH JAN

SATURDAY 5TH JAN

3. What is the name of the inverted mountain home of the dragon riders, first encountered in *The Colour of Magic*?

☞ ------------------------

SUNDAY 6TH JAN

Epiphany

OCTEDA

YOUR BONUS FOR 3 POINTS!

4. Along with Tubul, Great T'Phon and Berilia, what is the name of the fourth elephant still standing atop Great A'Tuin's meteor-pocked shell?

☞ ------------------------------------

YOUR SCORE SO FAR: ______

MONDAY 7TH JAN

5. Granny Weatherwax is most famous for her use of what style of magic?

☞ ______________________

TUESDAY 8TH JAN

WEDNESDAY 9TH JAN

6. When shall we three meet again?

☞ __________________

THURSDAY 10TH JAN

ANSWERS

5. *Headology*
6. *Well, I can do next Tuesday*
7. *Lily Weatherwax AKA Lilith de Tempscire*
8. *Tir Nani Ogg, Lit. Trans. 'Nanny Ogg's Place'*

FRIDAY 11TH JAN

SATURDAY 12TH JAN

7. What is the name of Esmerelda Weatherwax's sister?

☞ ____________________

SUNDAY 13TH JAN

OCTEDA

YOUR BONUS FOR 3 POINTS!

8. What is the name of Nanny Ogg's Lancre town house?

☞ ____________________

YOUR SCORE SO FAR: ______

MONDAY 14TH JAN

TUESDAY 15TH JAN

9. How often do 'million-to-one chances' occur?

☞ ______________________

WEDNESDAY 16TH JAN

THURSDAY 17TH JAN

10. According to the Discworld proverb, what can the leopard not change?

☞ ______________________

ANSWERS

9. *Nine times out of ten*
10. *His shorts* **11.** *Minute*
12. *Bloody Furious – just ask Greebo after Champot locks him in a box*

FRIDAY 18TH JAN

11. According to Discworld logic, 'There's always time for one more last ___'?

☞ ------------------------

SATURDAY 19TH JAN

SUNDAY 20TH JAN

OCTEDA...

YOUR BONUS FOR 3 POINTS!

12. If a cat in a box is unobserved, it has three possible states of being; it could be Alive, Dead and/or which other state ___ ___?

☞ ------------------------

YOUR SCORE SO FAR: ______

- FOOD & DRINK -

MONDAY 21ST JAN

13. Which dwarfish delicacy is best served 'onna-stick'?

☞ ------------------------

TUESDAY 22ND JAN

WEDNESDAY 23RD JAN

14. From which establishment does Death prefer to get his Klatchian takeaway?

☞ ------------------------

THURSDAY 24TH JAN

ANSWERS

13. *Rat (with ketchup of course!)*
14. *Curry Gardens in Ankh-Morpork*
15. *Dwarf Bread*
16. *Egg, soss and bacon with a fried slice*

FRIDAY 25TH JAN

SATURDAY 26TH JAN

15. In Whirligig Avenue there is a museum dedicated to which 'food'?

☞ ____________________________

Australia Day

SUNDAY 27TH JAN

OCTEDA

YOUR BONUS FOR 3 POINTS!

16. Not ones for fancy or exotic cuisine, Morporkians prefer conventional foods, like flightless bird embryos, minced organs in intestine skins, slices of hog flesh and burnt ground grass seeds dipped in animal fats. What is this dish better known as?

☞ ____________________________

YOUR SCORE SO FAR: ________

C.M.O.T. DIBBLER

MONDAY 28TH JAN

TUESDAY 29TH JAN

17. In *Jingo*, Solid Jackson was out fishing for which sea-beastie when he discovered the island of Leshp?

☞ ______________________

WEDNESDAY 30TH JAN

THURSDAY 31ST JAN

18. Which species can boast the Disc's greatest mathematician?

☞ ______________________

ANSWERS

17. *Curious Squid*
18. *You Bastard, the greatest mathematician, is a CAMEL* **19.** *The Quantum Weather Butterfly*
20. *The Lancre Woodwasp*

FRIDAY 1ST FEB

Beating the Bounds (Plunkers)

SATURDAY 2ND FEB

Imbolc (Candlemas)

SUNDAY 3RD FEB

19. Causing meteorological chaos with its infinite, fractal-edged wings, by which name is Papilio Tempestae otherwise known?

☞ ----------------------------

YOUR BONUS FOR 3 POINTS!

20. By what other name would Lancrastians know the Lappet-Faced Worrier?

☞ ----------------------------------

YOUR SCORE SO FAR: ________

MONDAY 4TH FEB

21. Ick, Offle and Grune are Discworldian examples of what?

☞ ______________________

TUESDAY 5TH FEB

WEDNESDAY 6TH FEB

22. How many seasons are there on the Discworld?

☞ ______________________

Accession of Queen Elizabeth II. Waitangi Day

THURSDAY 7TH FEB

ANSWERS

***21.** Calendar months*
***22.** Eight – Spring Prime, Summer, Autumn Prime, Spindlewinter (Winter Secundus), Secundus Spring, Summer Two, Secundus Autumn and Backspindlewinter*
***23.** Small Gods* ***24.** 800 days (in order to distribute the weight fairly upon its supportive pachyderms, according to Reforgule of Krull)*

FRIDAY 8TH FEB

SATURDAY 9TH FEB

23. In which book do the History Monks first appear?

☞ ---------------------

SUNDAY 10TH FEB

OCTEDA

YOUR BONUS FOR 3 POINTS!

24. How many days does it take for the Disc to revolve once?

☞ ---------------------------------

YOUR SCORE SO FAR: ______

MONDAY 11TH FEB

TUESDAY 12TH FEB

25. Whose unfinished autobiography is entitled *Along the Ankh with Bow, Rod and Staff with a Knob on the End*?

☞ ------------------------

WEDNESDAY 13TH FEB

THURSDAY 14TH FEB

26. What is the title of Twoflower's book, describing the events of *The Colour of Magic*?

☞ ------------------------

ANSWERS

25. *Mustrum Ridcully*

26. *What I did on my Holidays*

27. *Gold*

28. *Sloshi – many clown battles can be a total whitewash!*

FRIDAY 15TH FEB

27. Can you complete this line from the traditional dwarf song: 'Gold, Gold, ___, Gold'?

☞ ------------------------

SATURDAY 16TH FEB

SUNDAY 17TH FEB

Septuagesima Sunday

OCTEDA

YOUR BONUS FOR 3 POINTS!

28. Which martial art is practiced by members of the Fools' Guild?

☞ ------------------------------

YOUR SCORE SO FAR: ______

MONDAY 18TH FEB

29. Which Lancre libation is made from 'mostly apples'?

☞ ------------------------

TUESDAY 19TH FEB

WEDNESDAY 20TH FEB

30. Whose menu includes Vermincelli, Pizza Quatro-Rodenti with extra newts and Soya Rat?

☞ ------------------------

THURSDAY 21ST FEB

ANSWERS

29. *Scumble – though we'd also accept Suicider!*
30. *Gimlet Gimlet, of Gimlet's Hole Food Delicatessen*
31. *Verity Pushpram* **32.** *The Mended/Broken Drum*

FRIDAY 22ND FEB

SATURDAY 23RD FEB

SUNDAY 24TH FEB

31. What's the name of the owner of the clam & cockle barrow in Rime Street (also object of Nobby Nobb's unrequited affections)?

☞ ------------------------------

Sexagesima Sunday

OCTEDA

YOUR BONUS FOR 3 POINTS!

32. Which famous Morporkian establishment was run by Broadman, and Hibiscus Dunelm?

☞ ------------------------------

YOUR SCORE SO FAR: ______

MONDAY 25TH FEB

33. In which mountain range is the kingdom of Lancre found?

☞ ______________________

TUESDAY 26TH FEB

WEDNESDAY 27TH FEB

THURSDAY 28TH FEB

34. The city of Zambingo is in which country?

☞ ______________________

ANSWERS

33. *The Ramtops*

34. *The Kingdom of Howondaland*

35. *The Zoons, Esk travels with them in Equal Rites*

37. *The Citadel, Omnia*

FRIDAY 1ST MAR

35. Which group of freshwater merchant mariners are typically incapable of lying?

☞ --------------------

St David's Day (Wales)

SATURDAY 2ND MAR

SUNDAY 3RD MAR

Quinquagesima Sunday

OCTEDAY

YOUR BONUS FOR 3 POINTS!

36. Where might one encounter Cut-Me-Own-Hand-Off Dhblah, purveyor of suspiciously new holy relics, gritty figs and long-past-their-sell-by dates?

☞ ------------------------------

YOUR SCORE SO FAR: ______

- ANAGRAMS -

The average human, if they're lucky, can expect to live for roughly 37,580,400 minutes. You're about to spend an inordinate amount of those unscrambling letters to reveal Discworld names, places and phrases. And why, we hear you ask?! In the pursuit of Discworld Trivia Points, of course!

If it makes you feel any better, our team of researchers spent some considerable time messing them all up too, so none of us come out of this looking terribly sensible. Rearrange the letters (disregarding their current spacing) to reveal the secret subject. *Answers on page* 124.

- CHARACTERS -

A) EVIL SEAS MUM

☞ ________________________________

B) VIOLIN WIG STOMP

☞ ________________________________

C) GO THY GAG

☞ ________________________________

D) A FANCY FIG THIN

☞ ________________________________

E) A HOSTED FART

☞ ________________________________

- PLACES -

F) UNSAFE MIND TIN

☞ ________________________________

G) ELK HATCH

☞ ________________________________

H) SHES HATED

☞ ________________________________

I) OTTER OF WAR

☞ ________________________________

J) SPOILED SOUP

☞ ________________________________

- BOOKS -

K) LACY TOFFEE

☞ ____________

L) JUMP LACE GURU

☞ ____________

M) WOW MS CHEERY

☞ ____________

N) A MANIAC NEEDS CLUES

☞ ____________

O) A TV TO ECHO

☞ ____________

- SPECIES -

P) GOB ENEMY

☞ ____________

Q) ROYAL EGGS

☞ ____________

R) CAGE FECAL MEN

☞ ____________

S) HAS BEEN

☞ ____________

T) SEWER VOWEL

☞ ____________

- ORGANISATIONS -

U) ELF CRABS THRUST

☞ ____________

V) TURTLE SMOG

☞ ____________

W) HUGE MONK TINGS

☞ ____________

X) MR INCREMENTAL HORSE

☞ ____________

Y) A FAECAL MONGERS THIGH QUIP

☞ ____________

ONE DISCWORLD TRIVIA POINT FOR EACH AND EVERY ANAGRAM DECIPHERED!

YOUR SCORE SO FAR: ______

MONDAY 4TH MAR

TUESDAY 5TH MAR

37. Which institution is largely staffed by 'interchangeable Emmas'?

☞ ________________________

WEDNESDAY 6TH MAR

Ash Wednesday

THURSDAY 7TH MAR

38. Complete the title of this ill-fated group of conspirators: the 'Elucidated Brethren of the ___ Night'?

☞ ________________________

ANSWERS

37. *The Sunshine Sanctuary for Sick Dragons* **38.** *Ebon* **39.** *Schleppel the bogeyman, he's got to have SOMETHING to hide behind!* **40.** *Chrysoprase*

FRIDAY 8TH MAR

39. Which member of The Fresh Start Club will often be found carrying a heavy wooden door?

☞ ------------------------

SATURDAY 9TH MAR

Samedi Nuit Mort

SUNDAY 10TH MAR

Quadragesima Sunday

TEDAY

YOUR BONUS FOR 3 POINTS!

40. In *Soul Music*, who is rumored to be a godfather in the Breccia, an Ankh-Morpork troll crime syndicate?

☞ --------------------------------

YOUR SCORE SO FAR: ______

MONDAY 11TH MAR

> **41.** Which guild is famously duty-bound to issue a receipt with each and every encounter?
>
> ☞ ________________________

Commonwealth Day

TUESDAY 12TH MAR

Creator's Day (GNU Terry Pratchett)

WEDNESDAY 13TH MAR

> **42.** Which guild house can be found above a barbers' shop on Tin Lid Alley?
>
> ☞ ________________________

THURSDAY 14TH MAR

ANSWERS

41. *The Thieves' Guild (or Guild of Thieves, Cutpurses, Housebreakers and Allied Trades if we're being picky)*
42. *The Musicians' Guild* **43.** *The Assassins' Guild school*
44. *The Gamblers' Guild (Lit. Trans. Shit out of luck)*

FRIDAY 15TH MAR

43. Lady T'Malia teaches 'Political Expediency' at which prestigious Ankh-Morpork guild school?

☞ ---------------------------

SATURDAY 16TH MAR

SUNDAY 17TH MAR

St Patrick's Day (Holiday Northern Ireland)

TEDAY

YOUR BONUS FOR 3 POINTS!

44. Which guild boasts the motto EXCRETUS EX FORTUNA?

☞ ---------------------------------

YOUR SCORE SO FAR: ______

MONDAY 18TH MAR

TUESDAY 19TH MAR

45. Which bloom has become synonymous with the Glorious 25th of May?

☞ ----------------------

WEDNESDAY 20TH MAR

Vernal Equinox – Spring begins

THURSDAY 21ST MAR

46. Which giant beings were trapped under the Hub by the gods, after the mage wars?

☞ ----------------------

ANSWERS

45. *Lilac* **46.** *The Ice Giants*
47. *Alberto Malich – Or Albert, as Death tends to call him* **48.** *Suffer-Not-Injustice Vimes – better known as 'Old Stoneface Vimes'*

FRIDAY 22ND MAR

SATURDAY 23RD MAR

47. Who founded the Unseen University well over a thousand years ago?

☞ ______________________

SUNDAY 24TH MAR

TEDAY

YOUR BONUS FOR 3 POINTS!

48. A statue stands right outside the Palace, remembering the killer of the last king of Ankh-Morpork. Who was this renegade?

☞ ______________________________

YOUR SCORE SO FAR: ________

MONDAY 25TH MAR

49. How is 'Dr A.A. Dinwiddie (with an 'O'), D.M.(7th), D.Thau., B.Occ., M.Coll., B.F.', better known?

☞ ______________________________

TUESDAY 26TH MAR

WEDNESDAY 27TH MAR

50. Which wizard was promoted to the position of Royal Recogniser of Sto Lat?

☞ ______________________

THURSDAY 28TH MAR

ANSWERS

49. *The Bursar*

50. *Igneous Cutwell*

51. *Eskarina Smith – the first female wizard at Unseen University*

52. *Mrs. Whitlow*

FRIDAY 29TH MAR

SATURDAY 30TH MAR

SUNDAY 31ST MAR

51. Which wizard, born in the Ramtops, went on to rescue Simon from the Dungeon Dimensions in *Equal Rites*?

☞ ------------------------------

Mothering Sunday

OCTEDA

YOUR BONUS FOR 3 POINTS!

52. Held in high regard (for a woman!), who is the head house-keeper at Unseen University?

☞ ------------------------------

YOUR SCORE SO FAR: ______

- FLORA AND FAUNA -

MONDAY 1ST APR

April Fool's Day

TUESDAY 2ND APR

53. Of which material does The Luggage primarily consist?

☞ ______________________

WEDNESDAY 3RD APR

THURSDAY 4TH APR

54. Which species of albatross is the messenger bird of choice for the Agatean Empire?

☞ ______________________

ANSWERS

53. *Sapient Pearwood*
54. *Pointless Albatross*
55. *Hodgesaargh!*
56. *The Ambiguous Puzuma*

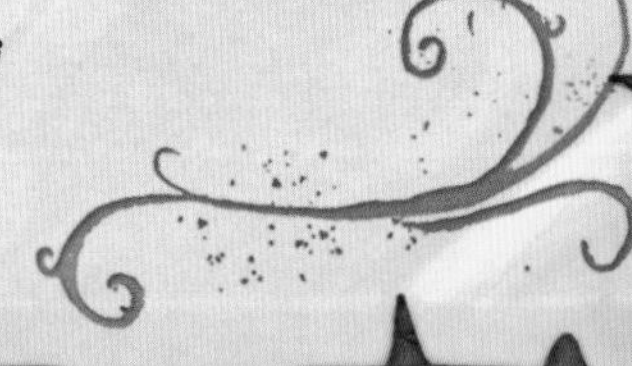

FRIDAY 5TH APR

55. What is the semi-onomatopoeic moniker of Lancre's, ahem, 'finest' falconer?

☞ ________________________

SATURDAY 6TH APR

SUNDAY 7TH APR

TEDAY

YOUR BONUS FOR 3 POINTS!

56. What is the fastest feline species on the face of the Disc?

☞ ________________________________

YOUR SCORE SO FAR: ______

MONDAY 8TH APR

TUESDAY 9TH APR

57. Which witch took on the cottage of her mentor, Goodie Whemper, in Mad Stoat?

☞ ______________________

WEDNESDAY 10TH APR

THURSDAY 11TH APR

58. Which member of the extensive Ogg clan is described as 'possibly the stickiest child in the world'?

☞ ______________________

ANSWERS

57. *Magrat Garlick*
58. *Pewsey Ogg*
59. *Granny Weatherwax*
60. *Ammeline 'Goodie' Hamstring*

FRIDAY 12TH APR

59. Who do the trolls of the Ramtops call 'Aaoograha hoa' (lit. trans. 'She Who Must Be Avoided')?

☞ ----------------------------

SATURDAY 13TH APR

SUNDAY 14TH APR

Palm Sunday

TEDAY

YOUR BONUS FOR 3 POINTS!

60. Which witch does Mort have to usher into the next world?

☞ ----------------------------------

YOUR SCORE SO FAR: ______

MONDAY 15TH APR

61. Of which species is Constable Downspout a proud member?

☞ ______________________

TUESDAY 16TH APR

WEDNESDAY 17TH APR

62. Which diminutive copper was the first member of Ankh-Morpork City Watch Airborne Section?

☞ ______________________

THURSDAY 18TH APR

61. *Gargoyles*
62. *Buggy Swires*
63. *Nobby*
64. *Delphine*

FRIDAY 19TH APR

Good Friday – Public Holiday UK

SATURDAY 20TH APR

63. By which first name is Cecil Wormsborough St John Nobbs better known?

☞ ----------------------

First Day of Passover (Pesach)

SUNDAY 21ST APR

Easter Day. Birthday of Queen Elizabeth II

TEDAY

YOUR BONUS FOR 3 POINTS!

64. What is Sgt Angua Von Uberwald's FIRST name?

☞ ----------------------------------

YOUR SCORE SO FAR: ______

MONDAY 22ND APR

Easter Monday. Public Holiday – England, Wales, Northern Ireland

TUESDAY 23RD APR

65. Left behind by the creator and containing the eight great spells, which is considered the most dangerous book on the Discworld?

☞ ------------------------------------

St George's Day (England)

WEDNESDAY 24TH APR

THURSDAY 25TH APR

66. What does a wizard's staff typically have on the end?

☞ ----------------------

ANZAC Day

ANSWERS

65. *The Octavo*

66. *A knob… no sniggering*

67. *It doesn't exist, to the mutual benefit of faculty and students alike*

68. *Old Tom*

FRIDAY 26TH APR

67. What is special about Room 3b, where most Unseen University lectures take place?

☞ ______________________

SATURDAY 27TH APR

SUNDAY 28TH APR

Low Sunday
Creator's Birthday (b.1948)

OCTEDA…

YOUR BONUS FOR 3 POINTS!

68. What's the name of the tongueless bell in the bell tower of Unseen University, which tolls tremendously sonorous silences every hour?

☞ ______________________

YOUR SCORE SO FAR: ______

– FILL IN THE -ING BLANKS –

The purpose of this exercise is to render each of the following phrases complete. It's difficult to quantify exactly how many words are in existence. It is suggested that, allowing for prefixed and suffixed words, colloquial dialects, differing tenses and slang, there are at LEAST a quarter of a million definable words in the English language. Either way, it is a comfort to know that this round can technically be considered multiple choice.

Select the correct word/s from the English language to complete the following phrases. *Answers on page* 124.

A) *Soul Music* 'Susan hated ________________. She'd much prefer to read a good book.'

B) *Small Gods* '______ are always a help in times of stress. And in times of starvation, too, of course.'

C) *Wyrd Sisters* 'A Wizard's Staff Has a _____ on The End.'

D) *Sourcery* "I meant,' said Ipslore bitterly, 'what is there in this world that makes living worthwhile?' Death thought about it. '______', he said eventually '______ARE NICE."

E) *Guards! Guards!* "______', said the Librarian.'

F) *Small Gods* 'It's a _____-eat-_____world.'

G) *Guards! Guards!* 'A good ________________ is just a genteel black hole that knows how to read.'

H) *Eric* "What're quantum ________________?' 'I don't know. People who repair quantums, I suppose."

I) *Soul Music* '______ duck?'

J) *Men at Arms* "THAT'S NOT UP TO ME.' Death coughed. 'OF COURSE … SINCE YOU BELIEVE IN REINCARNATION … ' 'YOU'LL BE ________ AGAIN."

K) *Colour of Magic* "My name is ________________,' she said. 'That's a pretty name,' said Rincewind."

L) *Soul Music* 'Bee there Orr Bee A ______________ Thyng.'

M) *Small Gods* '________ is a drug. Too much of it kills you.'

N) *Equal Rites* 'The entire universe has been neatly divided into things to (a) mate with, (b) eat, (c) run away from, and (d) __________.'

O) *Moving Pictures* 'He gave Gaspode a long, slow stare, which was like challenging a _________________ to an arse-kicking contest.'

P) *Lords and Ladies* 'Nanny Ogg looked under her bed in case there was a _______ there. Well, you never knew your luck.'

Q) *Jingo* '________________, gentlemen, is very much like dairy farming. The task is to extract the maximum amount of milk with the minimum amount of moo.'

R) *Men at Arms* 'Corporal Nobbs had been disqualified from the human race for _________________.'

S) *The Light Fantastic* "... There was a whole bunch of people across the street helping themselves to musical instruments, can you believe that?' – 'Yeah,' said Rincewind. '...__________, I expect."

T) *Eric* 'Just erotic. Nothing kinky. It's the difference between using a feather and using a _______________.'

U) *Feet of Clay* 'It is the ancient instinct of terriers and _______________ to chase anything that runs away.'

YOU MAY AWARD YOURSELF ONE DISCWORLD TRIVIA POINT FOR EACH PHRASE CORRECTLY COMPLETED!

YOUR SCORE SO FAR: ________

MONDAY 29TH APR

69. King Gurnt The Stupid of Lancre once planned an aerial attack force which never quite got off the ground. Which armoured avians failed to fly?

☞ ---------------------------------------

TUESDAY 30TH APR

WEDNESDAY 1ST MAY

May Day
May Morning

THURSDAY 2ND MAY

70. Whose guide to peerage famously provides the most thorough record of Discworld nobility?

☞ ---------------------------------------

ANSWERS

***69.** Ravens – giving them plate armour may have been a mistake*

***70.** Twurp – it is imaginatively titled Twurp's Peerage* ***71.** Kring* ***72.** The Beggars' Guild – 'Now here,' said Carrot, 'is the Beggars' Guild. They're the oldest of the Guilds. Not many people know that.' – Men at Arms. (not to be mistaken for the 'oldest profession'!)*

FRIDAY 3RD MAY

71. Rincewind briefly wields which talking, singing (and whining) sword, as previously owned by Pasha of Redurant, the Archmandrite of B'Ituni, and Hrun the Barbarian?

☞ --

SATURDAY 4TH MAY

SUNDAY 5TH MAY

OCTEDAY

YOUR BONUS FOR 3 POINTS!

72. What is the oldest guild in Ankh-Morpork?

☞ --

YOUR SCORE SO FAR: ______

MONDAY 6TH MAY

First day of Ramadan. Early Spring Bank Public Holiday UK

TUESDAY 7TH MAY

73. What's the name of the stone circle found deep in the kingdom of Lancre, made of magnetic meteoric rocks?

☞ ----------------------------

WEDNESDAY 8TH MAY

THURSDAY 9TH MAY

74. What meteorological phenomenon might be seen lighting up the skies over Cori Celeste at the hub of the Disc?

☞ ----------------------------

ANSWERS

73. *The Dancers*
74. *The Aurora Coriolis AKA the Hublights* ***75.*** *The Agatean Empire (although it's now known as the People's Beneficent Republic of Agatea)* ***76.*** *Wincanton, home of the Discworld Emporium*

FRIDAY 10TH MAY

75. Which empire is situated on the Counterweight Continent?

☞ ______________________

SATURDAY 11TH MAY

SUNDAY 12TH MAY

OCTEDA

YOUR BONUS FOR 3 POINTS!

76. Which small town in the United Kingdom is officially twinned with Ankh-Morpork?

☞ ______________________

YOUR SCORE SO FAR: ______

MONDAY 13TH MAY

77. In *Small Gods*, in which manifestation is The Great God Om stuck?

☞ ---------------------------

TUESDAY 14TH MAY

WEDNESDAY 15TH MAY

78. Who is the Oh God of Hangovers?

☞ ------------------------

THURSDAY 16TH MAY

ANSWERS

77. *A very pissed-off tortoise*
78. *Bilious* ***79.*** *Rocks*
80. *Quezovercoatl ... accounting for three whole homicidal maniacs in one god*

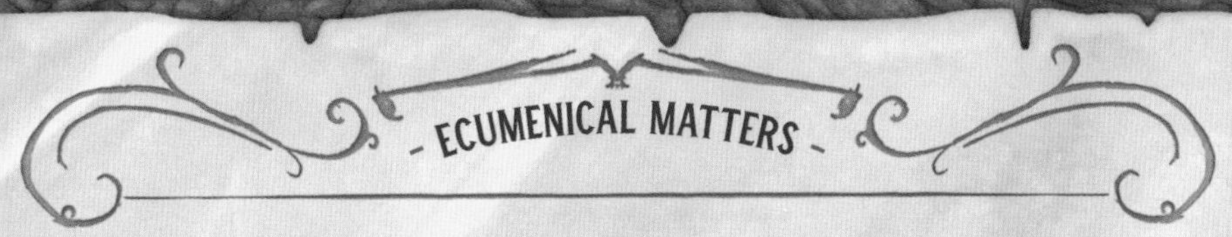

FRIDAY 17TH MAY

SATURDAY 18TH MAY

79. What is the missing word in the title of this ecumenical authority: Council of Churches, Temples, Sacred Groves and Big Ominous ___?

☞ ------------------------------------

SUNDAY 19TH MAY

TEDAY

YOUR BONUS FOR 3 POINTS!

80. Which god of the Tezuman Empire is described as 'Half man, half chicken, half jaguar, half serpent, half scorpion and half mad'?

☞ ------------------------------------

YOUR SCORE SO FAR: ______

MONDAY 20TH MAY

TUESDAY 21ST MAY

81. On which continent might you find the elusive 'Drop Bear'?

☞ ________________________

WEDNESDAY 22ND MAY

THURSDAY 23RD MAY

82. Who is the devoted owner of a small elderly wire-haired terrier called Wuffles?

☞ ____________________________

ANSWERS

81. *XXXX, Fourecks, The Last Continent, Terror Incognita … call it what you will, the Drop Bear calls it home* **82.** *Havelock Vetinari* **83.** *The .303 Bookworm* **84.** *Critters*

FRIDAY 24TH MAY

83. Which critter eats magical books, often so fast it ricochets off the walls of Unseen University Library?

☞ ---------------------------

SATURDAY 25TH MAY

The Glorious 25th of May

SUNDAY 26TH MAY

Rogation Sunday

TEDAY

YOUR BONUS FOR 3 POINTS!

84. Which species dwells in L-Space, grazing on the contents of the choicer books and leaving behind them piles of small slim volumes of literary criticism?

☞ ---------------------------

YOUR SCORE SO FAR: ______

MONDAY 27TH MAY

85. Which musician's name translates from his native Llamedosian language as 'bud of the holly'?

☞ ____________________________

Spring Bank Holiday UK

TUESDAY 28TH MAY

WEDNESDAY 29TH MAY

86. In *Moving Pictures*, which Holy Wood 'click' could be a Discworld parallel of Roundworld's *Gone with the Wind*?

☞ ____________________________

THURSDAY 30TH MAY

Ascension Day – Holy Thursday

ANSWERS

85. *Imp Y Celyn* **86.** *Blown Away!*
87. *Hwel* **88.** *The Reeling Rocks*
(The Whom clearly reference The Who, The Surreptitious Fabric mimics the Velvet Underground and Suck mirror KISS ... whereas The Reeling Rocks clearly don't match any known band...)

FRIDAY 31ST MAY

SATURDAY 1ST JUN

87. The *Taming of the Vole* is just one of the masterworks of which Discworld Playwright?

☞ ______________________

SUNDAY 2ND JUN

Coronation Day

YOUR BONUS FOR 3 POINTS!

88. Which of the following was NOT a band during the Soul Music craze; The Whom, The Reeling Rocks, The Surreptitious Fabric or Suck?

☞ ______________________

YOUR SCORE SO FAR: ________

MONDAY 3RD JUN

TUESDAY 4TH JUN

89. Which river in Lancre runs below Lancre Town, through Lancre Gorge and under Lancre Bridge?

☞ ---------------------------

WEDNESDAY 5TH JUN

THURSDAY 6TH JUN

90. Which major crocodile-infested river runs through the kingdom of Djelibeybi?

☞ ---------------------------

ANSWERS

89. *Lancre River … cartographic nomenclature isn't high on the list of Lancrastian priorities* **90.** *The Djel – Djelibeybi = child of the Djel* **91.** *Bad Ass* **92.** *Ella Saturday, since the events of Witches Abroad*

FRIDAY 7TH JUN

91. What's the unfortunate name of the Ramtops village in which Eskarina Smith was born?

☞ ----------------------------

SATURDAY 8TH JUN

The Queen's Official Birthday

SUNDAY 9TH JUN

Feast of Weeks (Shavuot). Whit Sunday – Pentecost

OCTEDA

YOUR BONUS FOR 3 POINTS!

92. Who is the reigning monarch of Genua?

☞ ----------------------------

YOUR SCORE SO FAR: ______

MONDAY 10TH JUN

Birthday of Prince Philip, Duke of Edinburgh

TUESDAY 11TH JUN

93. Which of these is NOT a known guild in Ankh-Moporok: Guild of Town Criers, Archaeologists' Guild, Conjurers' Guild or Guild of Flagmakers?

☞ ----------------------------------

WEDNESDAY 12TH JUN

THURSDAY 13TH JUN

94. Which Ankh-Morpork civic body fights to stop people looking down on dwarfs and belittling their plight?

☞ ----------------------------------

ANSWERS

93. *Flagmakers*
94. *The Campaign for Equal Heights*
95. *The Fools' Guild (Lit. Trans. I say, I say, I say)*
96. *Silicon Anti-Defamation League*

FRIDAY 14TH JUN

95. 'Dico, Dico, Dico' is the motto of which of Ankh-Morpork's guilds?

☞ ________________

SATURDAY 15TH JUN

SUNDAY 16TH JUN

Trinity Sunday

OCTEDA[illegible]

YOUR BONUS FOR 3 POINTS!

96. Which civic body looks after the concerns of trolls and 'come down like a ton of rectangular building things' on any troll acting out?

☞ ________________

YOUR SCORE SO FAR: ________

MONDAY 17TH JUN

97. The Great Gates of Unseen University are an imposing feature of which public square?

☞ ------------------------

TUESDAY 18TH JUN

Small Gods' Eve

WEDNESDAY 19TH JUN

Small Gods' Day

THURSDAY 20TH JUN

98. Which prominent 'power couple' lives in Scoone Avenue?

☞ ------------------------

Corpus Christi

ANSWERS

97. *Sator Square*

98. *The Vimes/Ramkin family*

99. *Lord Havelock Vetinari* **100.** *Wherever Mr Scant is, he keeps it in a small cardboard box in his pocket*

FRIDAY 21ST JUN

Summer Solstice – Summer begins

SATURDAY 22ND JUN

99. In Ankh-Morpork's 'One Man, One Vote' take on democracy – who gets the vote?

☞ ------------------------

SUNDAY 23RD JUN

OCTEDA

YOUR BONUS FOR 3 POINTS!

100. Where in Ankh-Morpork is Bloody Stupid Johnson's Triumphal Arch?

☞ ------------------------------------

YOUR SCORE SO FAR: ______

- OPENING LINES -

Identify these Discworld novels by their opening lines. *Answers on page* 124.

A) 'In a distant and second-hand set of dimensions, in an astral plane that was never meant to fly, the curling star-mists waver and part ... See ... Great A'Tuin the turtle comes.'

☞ ------------------------------

B) 'Everything starts somewhere, although many physicists disagree.'

☞ ------------------------------

C) 'The Morris dance is common to all inhabited worlds in the multiverse. It is danced under blue skies to celebrate the quickening of the soil and under bare stars because it's springtime and with any luck the carbon dioxide will unfreeze again. The imperative is felt by deep-sea beings who have never seen the sun and urban humans whose only connection with the cycles of nature is that their Volvo once ran over a sheep.'

☞ ------------------------------

D) 'This is where the gods play games with the lives of men, on a board which is at one and the same time a simple playing area and the whole world. And Fate always wins.'

☞ ------------------------------

E) 'The wind howled. The storm crackled on the mountains. Lightning prodded the crags like an old man trying to get an elusive blackberry pip out of his false teeth. Among the hissing furze bushes a fire blazed, the flames driven this way and that by the gusts. An eldritch voice shrieked: 'When shall we ... two ... meet again?"

☞ ------------------------------

F) 'Now consider the tortoise and the eagle.'

☞ ------------------------------

G) 'The bees of Death are big and black, they buzz low and sombre, they keep their honey in combs of wax as white as altar candles. The honey is black as night, thick as sin and sweet as treacle.'

☞ ------------------------------

H) 'The sun rose slowly, as if it wasn't sure it was worth all the effort. Another Disc day dawned, but very gradually, and this is why. When light encounters a strong magical field it loses all sense of urgency. It slows right down.'

☞ ------------------------------

I) 'This is a story about magic and where it goes and perhaps more importantly where it comes from and why, although it doesn't pretend to answer all or any of these questions. It may, however, help to explain why Gandalf never got married.'

☞ ------------------------------

J) 'This is where the dragons went. They lie … Not dead, not asleep. Not waiting, because waiting implies expectation. Possibly the word we're looking for here is … dormant.'

☞ ------------------------------

K) 'This is the bright candlelit room where the life-timers are stored – shelf upon shelf of them.'

☞ ------------------------------

L) 'Watch… This is space. It's sometimes called the final frontier. (Except that of course you can't have a final frontier, because there'd be nothing for it to be a frontier to, but as frontiers go, it's pretty penultimate …)'

☞ ------------------------------

M) 'There was a man and he had eight sons. Apart from that, he was nothing more than a comma on the page of History. It's sad, but that's all you can say about some people.'

☞ ------------------------------

N) 'The wind howled. Lightning stabbed at the earth erratically, like an ineffcient assassin. Thunder rolled back and forth across the dark, rain-lashed hills. The night was as black as the inside of a cat.'

☞ ------------------------------

O) 'It was a moonless night, which was good for the purposes of Solid Jackson. He fished for Curious Squid … '

☞ ------------------------------

P) 'It was a warm spring night when a fist knocked at the door so hard that the hinges bent. A man opened it and peered out into the street. There was mist coming off the river and it was a cloudy night. He might as well have tried to see through white velvet. But he thought afterwards that there had been shapes out there, just beyond the light spilling out into the road. A lot of shapes, watching him carefully. He thought maybe there'd been very faint points of light … '

☞ ------------------------------

One Discworld Trivia Point for Each Correct Answer!

Your Score So Far: ______

MONDAY 24TH JUN

101. Which of these is not a troll drug: Slab, Swinge, Sleek, Crystal Slam?

☞ ----------------------------

Treacle Pie Day

TUESDAY 25TH JUN

WEDNESDAY 26TH JUN

102. Which pastry-covered raisin treat is it apparently disagreeable to be hung by, have toasted or be placed upon a spike?

☞ ----------------------------

THURSDAY 27TH JUN

ANSWERS

101. *Swinge (which is actually one of Gaspode's myriad collection of diseases)* ***102.*** *Your figgin* ***103.*** *Learn The Words* ***104.*** *Zebbo Mooty*

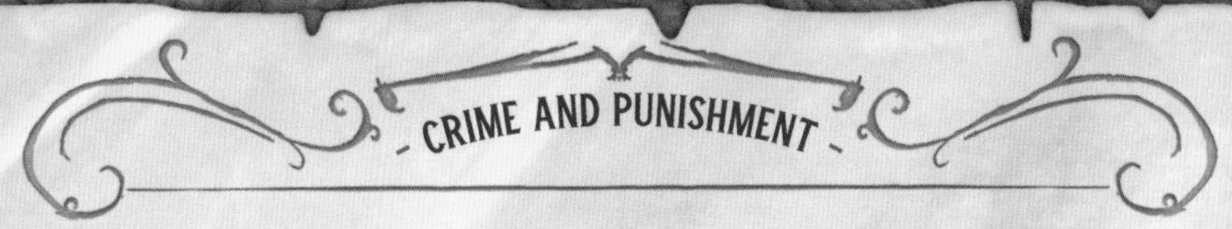

FRIDAY 28TH JUN

SATURDAY 29TH JUN

Wizards' Excuse Me, end of Backspindle Term

SUNDAY 30TH JUN

103. Any mime artist found operating within Ankh-Morpork's crumbling city walls would quickly find themselves in the scorpion pit, on the wall of which is painted which piece of advice from Lord Vetinari?

☞ --

OCTEDA

YOUR BONUS FOR 3 POINTS!

104. Which thief (third class) whilst attempting a mugging was the first person to be incinerated by dragon fire in hundreds of years?

☞ --

YOUR SCORE SO FAR: ______

- CITY LIFE -

MONDAY 1ST JUL

Canada Day

TUESDAY 2ND JUL

105. Which species, described by Terry as a variety of 'stone goblin', can be found cleaning the streets of Ankh-Morpork or in the employ of Harry King?

☞ ---------------------------------

WEDNESDAY 3RD JUL

THURSDAY 4TH JUL

106. By which name is Lord Vetinari's rectangular office known?

☞ ---------------------------------

Independence Day

ANSWERS

105. *Gnolls – Sometimes known as Grassy Gnolls due to the compost they carry on their backs* **106.** *The Oblong Office* **107.** *Misbegot Bridge* **108.** *We Can Rule You Wholesale*

FRIDAY 5TH JUL

107. Which Ankh-Morpork bridge is home to The Canting Crew?

☞ ---------------------------

SATURDAY 6TH JUL

Patrician's Day

SUNDAY 7TH JUL

OCTEDA

YOUR BONUS FOR 3 POINTS!

108. What is the name of Ankh-Morpork's national anthem, beginning 'When dragons belch and hippos flee, My thoughts, Ankh-Morpork, are of thee'?

☞ ---------------------------

YOUR SCORE SO FAR: ______

ECUMENICAL MATTERS

MONDAY 8TH JUL

109. What might one sacrifice as an offering to Offler, the Crocodile God?

☞ ---------------------------

TUESDAY 9TH JUL

WEDNESDAY 10TH JUL

THURSDAY 11TH JUL

110. Who is the god of 'small animals whose ultimate destiny is to be an abrupt damp squeak'?

☞ ---------------------------

ANSWERS

***109.** Sausages! That's the way to do it!* ***110.** Herne the hunted* ***111.** Things that get stuck in drawers* ***112.** Volcanoes – her constantly smouldering cigarette is a vestige of this role*

FRIDAY 12TH JUL

Battle of the Boyne (Holiday Northern Ireland)

SATURDAY 13TH JUL

SUNDAY 14TH JUL

111. What is Anoia currently the goddess of?

☞ ________________

Bastille Day

OCTEDA

YOUR BONUS FOR 3 POINTS!

112. What was Anoia originally the goddess of?

☞ ________________

YOUR SCORE SO FAR: ______

MONDAY 15TH JUL

TUESDAY 16TH JUL

113. By which name are the duo Dotsie and Sadie better known?

☞ ________________________

WEDNESDAY 17TH JUL

THURSDAY 18TH JUL

114. The De Bris gang is chiefly made up of which species?

☞ ________________________

ANSWERS

113. *The Agony Aunts*
114. *Trolls!*
115. *Detritus*
116. *Dorfl, the Golem*

FRIDAY 19TH JUL

SATURDAY 20TH JUL

SUNDAY 21ST JUL

115. Which Watchman is the splatter (like a bouncer, but with more ... emphasis) at the Mended Drum when first we meet him?

☞ ------------------------------

TEDAY

YOUR BONUS FOR 3 POINTS!

116. To whom does the phrase 'We can rebuild him, we have the pottery' apply?

☞ ------------------------------

YOUR SCORE SO FAR: ______

MONDAY 22ND JUL

Uberwald League of Temperance Day. Remember 'Not One Drop'

TUESDAY 23RD JUL

117. How many hands are usually appropriated to the god 'Sek'?

☞ ________________________

WEDNESDAY 24TH JUL

THURSDAY 25TH JUL

118. According to Sir Terry, who is the Goddess of Narrative?

☞ ________________________

ANSWERS

117. *Seven* **118.** *Narrativia (Also the name of the production company he founded with daughter Rhianna and business Manager Rob Wilkins.)* **119.** *Fedecks* **120.** *Petulia*

FRIDAY 26TH JUL

119. What is the messenger of the gods better known as?

☞ ___________________

SATURDAY 27TH JUL

SUNDAY 28TH JUL

De Murforte Day. Mizzling Sunday. Guild of Thieves Sports Day

TEDAY

YOUR BONUS FOR 3 POINTS!

120. Who is the patron deity of Seamstresses, to whom there have been some very (ahem) realistic statues (ahem) erected in Ephebe?

☞ ___________________

YOUR SCORE SO FAR: ______

- READING ORDER -

This task is really very simple. All you need to do is to put all forty-one of the major Discworld novels in order of publication. Fascinatingly, for the order of forty-one novels, there are only 33,452,526,613,163,807,108,170,062,053, 440,751,665,152,000,000,000 possible combinations, so you stand a chance. *Answers on page* 124.

Pyramids

Thief of Time

Mort

The Shepherd's Crown

Sourcery

Lords and Ladies

Witches Abroad

~~Faust~~ Eric

Soul Music

Reaper Man

The Light Fantastic

Small Gods

Moving Pictures

Wyrd Sisters

Guards! Guards!

The Colour of Magic

Carpe Jugulum

The Fifth Elephant

Equal Rites

Monstrous Regiment

Going Postal

Men at Arms

The Last Hero

I Shall Wear Midnight

Hogfather

Jingo

Thud!

Feet of Clay

Raising Steam

The Amazing Maurice and his Educated Rodents

Maskerade

Making Money

A Hat Full of Sky

Interesting Times

Wintersmith

The Wee Free Men

The Last Continent

Unseen Academicals

Night Watch

Snuff

The Truth

1) ☞ ______________________________

2) ☞ ______________________________

3) ☞ ______________________________

4) ☞ ______________________________

5) ☞ ______________________________

6) ☞ ______________________________

7) ☞ ______________________________

8) ☞ ______________________________

9) ☞ ______________________________

10) ☞ ______________________________

11) ☞ ______________________________

12) ☞ ______________________________

13) ☞ ______________________________

14) ☞ ______________________________

15) ☞ ______________________________

16) ☞ ______________________________

17) ☞ ______________________________

18) ☞ ______________________________

19) ☞ ______________________________

20) ☞ ______________________________

21) ☞ ______________________________

22) ☞ ______________________________

23) ☞ ______________________________

24) ☞ ______________________________

25) ☞ ______________________________

26) ☞ ______________________________

27) ☞ ______________________________

28) ☞ ______________________________

29) ☞ ______________________________

30) ☞ ______________________________

31) ☞ ______________________________

32) ☞ ______________________________

33) ☞ ______________________________

34) ☞ ______________________________

35) ☞ ______________________________

36) ☞ ______________________________

37) ☞ ______________________________

38) ☞ ______________________________

39) ☞ ______________________________

40) ☞ ______________________________

41) ☞ ______________________________

EACH BOOK YOU CORRECTLY NUMBER WILL NET YOU ONE DISCWORLD TRIVIA POINT!

YOUR SCORE SO FAR: ______

MONDAY 29TH JUL

121. Which is the sharpest object in the Discworld series, capable of slicing air, shadows and even time?

☞ ____________________________

TUESDAY 30TH JUL

WEDNESDAY 31ST JUL

THURSDAY 1ST AUG

122. Can you complete the title of the The Lancre Morris Men's famed favourite, 'The Stick and ___' dance?

☞ ____________________________

Lammas (Lughnasadh)

ANSWERS

***121.** Death's scythe ... we'd also accept Death's sword or Adora Belle's tongue* ***122.** Bucket!* ***123.** Lavatory paper* ***124.** Glod, after this poor dwarf was replicated some 2,000 times, the spell wore off*

FRIDAY 2ND AUG

SATURDAY 3RD AUG

123. According to Ghenghiz Cohen the greatest things in life are 'Hot water, good dentishtry and shoft ___ ___'?

☞ ----------------------------

SUNDAY 4TH AUG

OCTEDAY

YOUR BONUS FOR 3 POINTS!

124. The Seriph of Aly-bi was once cursed by a badly educated deity, everything he touched turned to ... what?

☞ ----------------------------------

YOUR SCORE SO FAR: ______

– WORST WIZZARD! –

MONDAY 5TH AUG

125. What word is written on Rincewind's hat?

☞ ---------------------------

August Bank Holiday (Scotland)

TUESDAY 6TH AUG

WEDNESDAY 7TH AUG

126. Once an assistant librarian, Rincewind's job title later becomes 'Egregious Professor of Cruel and Unusual __'?

☞ ------------------------

THURSDAY 8TH AUG

ANSWERS

***125.** Wizzard! (He can't 'spell')*
***126.** Geography* ***127.** One of the eight Great Spells left behind by the Creator, jumped from the pages of the Octavo into his head. It scares off any new spell Rincewind tries to put in there* ***128** The Small Boring Group of Faint Stars*

FRIDAY 9TH AUG

SATURDAY 10TH AUG

SUNDAY 11TH AUG

127. What resided in Rincewind's brain, which prevented him from learning new spells?

☞ ________________________

OCTEDA

YOUR BONUS FOR 3 POINTS!

128. What star sign was Rincewind born under?

☞ ________________________

YOUR SCORE SO FAR: ________

MONDAY 12TH AUG

129. What can the harvest hope for, if not for the care of the ___ ___?

☞ ________________________

TUESDAY 13TH AUG

WEDNESDAY 14TH AUG

THURSDAY 15TH AUG

130. What is the name of Death's trusted white steed?

☞ ________________________

ANSWERS

129. *Reaper Man*
130. *Binky*
131. KNEES *(capital letters or else!)* **132.** *Azrael, the Great Attractor, the Death of Universes, the beginning and end of time*

FRIDAY 16TH AUG

SATURDAY 17TH AUG

SUNDAY 18TH AUG

131. Complete the quote: "I WASN'T CUT OUT TO BE A FATHER, AND CERTAINLY NOT A GRANDAD. I HAVEN'T GOT THE RIGHT KIND OF __."

☞ --

OCTED

YOUR BONUS FOR 3 POINTS!

132. If Death talks LIKE THIS, who speaks LIKE THIS?

☞ --

YOUR SCORE SO FAR: ______

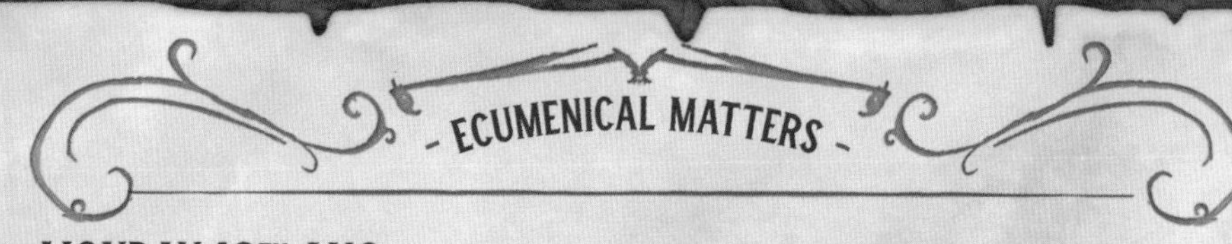

- ECUMENICAL MATTERS -

MONDAY 19TH AUG

133. Which blindfolded deity is currently considered chief of the gods?

☞ ____________________________

TUESDAY 20TH AUG

WEDNESDAY 21ST AUG

134. Flatulus is the chief deity of which elemental function?

☞ ____________________________

THURSDAY 22ND AUG

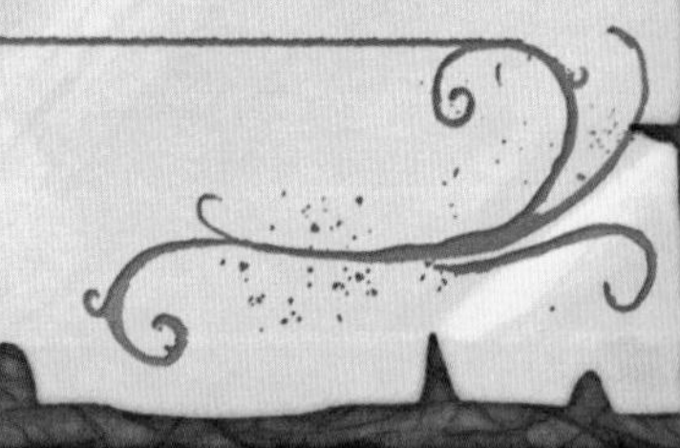

ANSWERS

133. *Blind Io*
134. *Wind*
135. *Omnian*
136. *Bel Shamharoth*

FRIDAY 23RD AUG

SATURDAY 24TH AUG

135. The Quite Reverent Mightily Oats is a representative of which religion?

☞ ----------------------------------

SUNDAY 25TH AUG

Head of the River

OCTEDA[illegible]

YOUR BONUS FOR 3 POINTS!

136. Which god is also known as Soul-Eater, the Soul-Render, and the Sender of Eight?

☞ ----------------------------------

YOUR SCORE SO FAR: ______

MONDAY 26TH AUG

Summer Bank Holiday – England, Wales, Northern Ireland

TUESDAY 27TH AUG

137. Whose precognitions can give her terrible headaches 'if'n people don't fill in the right bits'?

☞ ---------------------------

Brebb and Leppis Day

WEDNESDAY 28TH AUG

THURSDAY 29TH AUG

138. Which former handmaiden is now queen of Djelibeybi?

☞ --------------------

ANSWERS

137. *Mrs (Evadne) Cake*
138. *Ptraci*
139. *Giamo Casanunda ... by his own admission, he may be No.2, but he tries harder* **140.** *Tethys/Tethis*

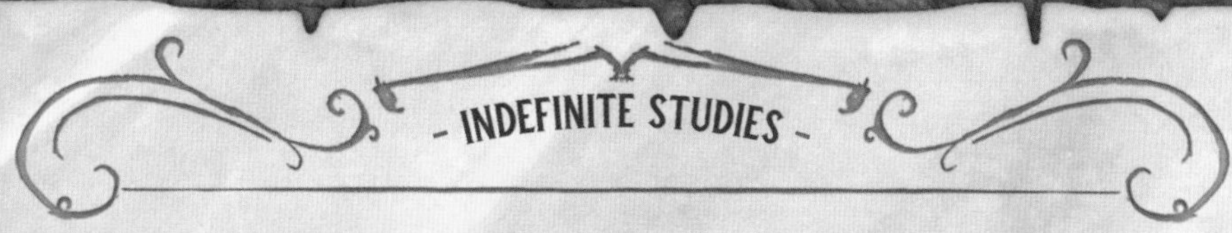

FRIDAY 30TH AUG

139. Who is the world's second greatest lover?

☞ ----------------------

SATURDAY 31ST AUG

Islamic New Year

SUNDAY 1ST SEP

OCTEDA

YOUR BONUS FOR 3 POINTS!

140. Which Sea Troll originally came to the Discworld from his home world Bathys?

☞ ----------------------------------

YOUR SCORE SO FAR: ______

MONDAY 2ND SEP

141. Carrot Ironfoundersson was raised in the mines under which mountain?

☞ ----------------------------

TUESDAY 3RD SEP

WEDNESDAY 4TH SEP

142. Where is the current Ankh-Morpork City Watch Headquarters found?

☞ ----------------------------

THURSDAY 5TH SEP

ANSWERS

141. *Copperhead*

142. *Pseudopolis Yard, Isle of Gods*

143. *Visit-the-Infidel-with-Explanatory-Pamphlets*

144. *Pantweed's Slim Panatellas*

FRIDAY 6TH SEP

SATURDAY 7TH SEP

SUNDAY 8TH SEP

143. Constable Visit is an evangelical Omnian, can you complete his given name: Visit-the-Infidel-with-___-___?

☞ ----------------------------

TEDAY

YOUR BONUS FOR 3 POINTS!

144. What brand of cigars does Sam Vimes prefer?

☞ ----------------------------------

YOUR SCORE SO FAR: ______

MONDAY 9TH SEP

145. By which other name is Goodboy Bindle Featherstone of Quirm known?

☞ ------------------------------

Rag Week Unseen University

TUESDAY 10TH SEP

WEDNESDAY 11TH SEP

THURSDAY 12TH SEP

146. Who is everyone's favourite Wonder Dog?

☞ ------------------------

ANSWERS

***145.** Errol, the swamp dragon*

***146.** Gaspode* ***147.** The Big Wahoonie*

***148.** The Hermit Elephant, it's not unknown for a traveler on the plains to wake up in the middle of a village that wasn't there yesterday*

FRIDAY 13TH SEP

SATURDAY 14TH SEP

147. Which malodourous fruit also serves as a nickname for Ankh-Morpork?

☞ ---------------------------------

SUNDAY 15TH SEP

OCTEDA

YOUR BONUS FOR 3 POINTS!

148. Which thin-skinned species makes its home in Howondalandian huts, moving up and building extensions as its size increases?

☞ ---------------------------------

YOUR SCORE SO FAR: ______

- TRUE OR FALSE? -

The French novelist Gustave Flaubert once wrote; 'There is no truth, there is only perception' ... The answers at the end of this round beg to differ.

We want you to channel your inner Watchman to help discern whether the following statements are fact or fiction ... well, technically they're all fiction ... but there ARE answers and they ARE final. *Answers on page* 125.

A) There is no mention of nettles in the entire Discworld cannon.

☐ **True** ☐ **False**

B) When Vetinari is taken ill in *Feet of Clay*, a horse doctor is called for.

☐ **True** ☐ **False**

C) Windle Poons was once the Archchancellor of Unseen University.

☐ **True** ☐ **False**

D) Followers of Offler the Crocodile God must carry votive peppermints at all times.

☐ **True** ☐ **False**

E) Death's horse is called Blinky.

☐ **True** ☐ **False**

F) Death loses Crippled Wa's floating crap game.

☐ **True** ☐ **False**

G) Dryads are never mentioned in the Discworld novels.

☐ **True** ☐ **False**

H) Nanny Ogg is the mother of Nev, Shawn and Wayne.

☐ **True** ☐ **False**

I) Lance-Constable Cuddy was killed during the events of *Men at Arms*.

☐ **True** ☐ **False**

J) Rincewind's full name is Rincewind Rincewind Rincewind.

☐ **True** ☐ **False**

K) Bravd the Hublander has the honour of being the first person to speak in the Discworld series.

☐ **True** ☐ **False**

L) The Yen Buddhists are the richest religious sect in the universe.

☐ **True** ☐ **False**

M) Leopold is the Oh God of Unwelcome Guests.

☐ **True** ☐ **False**

N) Denizens of Lancre are most commonly known as Lancrastians.

☐ **True** ☐ **False**

O) Ponder Stibbons is a student wizard at the beginning of *Moving Pictures.*

☐ **True** ☐ **False**

P) The Plaza of Broken Moons is in Quirm.

☐ **True** ☐ **False**

Q) No official member of the Beggars' Guild is ever mentioned by name.

☐ **True** ☐ **False**

R) The authorship of *The Light Fantastic* is officially credited as a collaboration.

☐ **True** ☐ **False**

S) The book *The Summoning of Dragons* is eventually returned to the Librarian.

☐ **True** ☐ **False**

T) Bugarup is a major city on the Counterweight Continent.

☐ **True** ☐ **False**

U) Errol the swamp dragon is killed by the Noble Dragon summoned in *Guards! Guards!*

☐ **True** ☐ **False**

V) Bergholt Stuttley 'Bloody Stupid' Johnson was killed by his own giant figgin.

☐ **True** ☐ **False**

W) There was once an Archchancellor Weatherwax at Unseen University.

☐ **True** ☐ **False**

X) Lord Vetinari was trained at the Lawyers' Guild.

☐ **True** ☐ **False**

Y) Evil-Minded Son of a Bitch is a camel in the click 'Shadowe of the Dessert'.

☐ **True** ☐ **False**

Z) Scumble is made from mostly apples.

☐ **True** ☐ **False**

AWARD YOURSELF ONE DISCWORLD TRIVIA POINT FOR EACH STATEMENT CORRECTLY IDENTIFIED AS BEING EITHER TRUE OR FALSE!

YOUR SCORE SO FAR: ______

MONDAY 16TH SEP

TUESDAY 17TH SEP

149. Which group of musicians is likely to have performed a song about 'Great Fiery Balls'?

☞ ____________________

WEDNESDAY 18TH SEP

THURSDAY 19TH SEP

150. Which of these is NOT a Discworld philosopher: Didactylos, Erysipelas, Orinjcrates or Legibus?

☞ ____________________

ANSWERS

149. *The Band with Rock In*
150. *Erysipelas (which is in fact a rather unpleasant skin condition)*
151. *The Dysc* **152.** *Barbarian Invaders*

FRIDAY 20TH SEP

151. Founded by Olwyn Vitoller in *Wyrd Sisters*, what is the name of Ankh-Morpork's favourite theatre?

☞ ______________________________

SATURDAY 21ST SEP

SUNDAY 22ND SEP

OCTEDA

YOUR BONUS FOR 3 POINTS!

152. In which clockwork bar-game might one find rows of little figures jerking and wobbling across a rectangular proscenium and dropping little metal arrows towards the player's self-loading catapult?

☞ ______________________________

YOUR SCORE SO FAR: ________

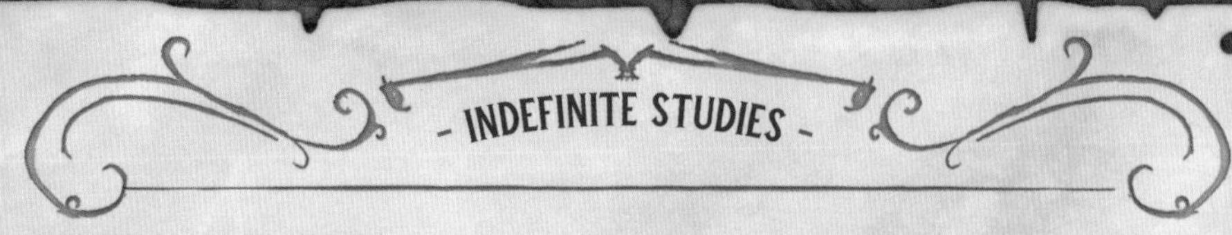

MONDAY 23RD SEP

153. By which name was Death known to Renata Flitworth?

☞ ____________________

Autumnal Equinox — Autumn begins

TUESDAY 24TH SEP

WEDNESDAY 25TH SEP

154. Which invention was named after Sir Charles Lavatory?

☞ ____________________

THURSDAY 26TH SEP

ANSWERS

153. *Bill Door*
154. *The Penny-whistle ... ok, it's actually the Lavatory. Sadly the invention of sewers is a little way off*
155. *5!!!!!* **156.** *King Murune. He didn't make friends easily*

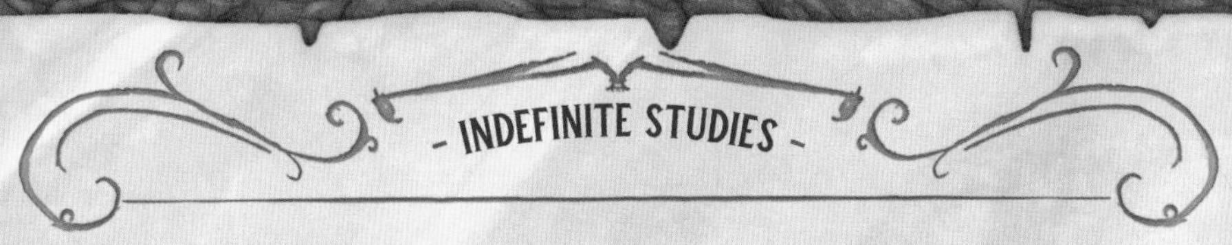

FRIDAY 27TH SEP

SATURDAY 28TH SEP

155. How many exclamation marks are the sign of an insane mind?

☞ ------------------------------

SUNDAY 29TH SEP

OCTEDA

YOUR BONUS FOR 3 POINTS!

156. Which former Lancre king's demise involved 'a red hot poker, ten pounds of live eels, a three mile stretch of frozen river, a butt of wine, a couple of tulip bulbs, a number of poisoned eardrops, an oyster and a large man with a mallet'?

☞ ------------------------------

YOUR SCORE SO FAR: ______

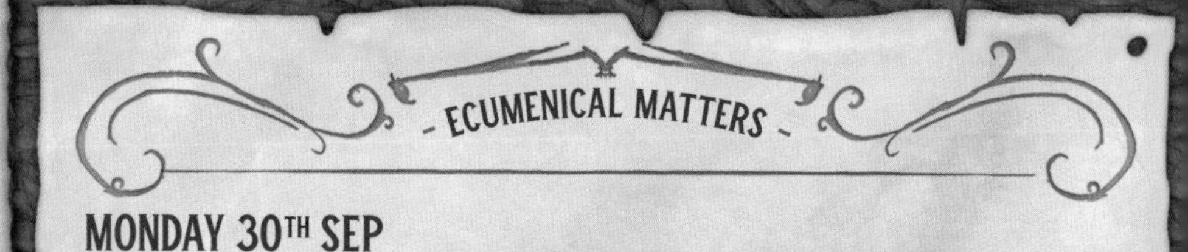

MONDAY 30TH SEP

Jewish New Year (Rosh Hashanah)

TUESDAY 1ST OCT

157. Which Deacon was the head of the Omnian Quisiton at the beginning of *Small Gods*?

☞ ________________________

WEDNESDAY 2ND OCT

THURSDAY 3RD OCT

158. The High Priest of Blind Io is also Mustrum Ridcully's brother. What is his name?

☞ ____________________________

ANSWERS

***157.** Deacon Vorbis*
***158.** Hughnon Ridcully*
***159.** A donkey*
***160.** Street of Small Gods, Ankh-Morpork*

FRIDAY 4TH OCT

159. Which species was the righteous ass, Holy St Bobby?

☞ ____________________

SATURDAY 5TH OCT

SUNDAY 6TH OCT

OCTEDA

YOUR BONUS FOR 3 POINTS!

160. On which street would you find The Temple of Blind Io, the Temple of Offler and the Temple of Seven-Handed Sek?

☞ ____________________

YOUR SCORE SO FAR: ________

MONDAY 7TH OCT

> **161.** According to Fred Colon, which part of a dragon must a would-be slayer hit?
>
> ☞ ________________________

TUESDAY 8TH OCT

Soul Cake Tuesday

WEDNESDAY 9TH OCT

Day of Atonement (Yom Kippur)

THURSDAY 10TH OCT

> **162.** Which Watchman is also known as Kzad-bhat (lit. tran. Head Banger)?
>
> ☞ ________________________

ANSWERS

161. *The 'Voonerables'*

162. *Carrot Ironfoundersson – what else would you call a 6ft dwarf in a 5ft mine?* **163.** *Cheri* **164.** *Beti, the somewhat grumpy exotic dancer. Collectively they are Gulli, Gulli and Beti*

FRIDAY 11TH OCT

SATURDAY 12TH OCT

163. Cheery Littlebottom is one of the first dwarfs (certainly in the Watch) to come out as female. Which name does she pick for herself?

☞ ________________________________

Chase Whiskers Day

SUNDAY 13TH OCT

TEDAY

YOUR BONUS FOR 3 POINTS!

164. What's the unlikely undercover identity of one Nobby Nobbs when he, Colon and Havelock Vetinari are forced to enter Klatchian territory during the events of *Jingo*?

☞ ________________________________

YOUR SCORE SO FAR: ______

MONDAY 14TH OCT

First day of Tabernacles (Succoth)

TUESDAY 15TH OCT

165. The Bursar of Unseen University takes pills to help him hallucinate that he is sane. Which pills are they?

☞ ------------------------------

WEDNESDAY 16TH OCT

THURSDAY 17TH OCT

166. Which wizard was temporarily laid to rest at the crossroads of Broadway and the Street of Small Gods?

☞ ------------------------------

B.E. Day

ANSWERS

165. *Dried Frog Pills*
166. *Windle Poons. It didn't work, but he appreciated the thought* **167.** *A thaumometer*
168. *Now you see it, now you don't!*

FRIDAY 18TH OCT

167. What instrument is used to measure the density of a magical field?

☞ ------------------------

SATURDAY 19TH OCT

SUNDAY 20TH OCT

OCTEDA

YOUR BONUS FOR 3 POINTS!

168. 'Nunc Id Vides, Nunc Ne Vides' is the Latatian official motto of Unseen University. What does it translate to in Morporkian?

☞ ------------------------

YOUR SCORE SO FAR: ______

– WHOSE LINE IS IT… EH? –

It is commonly agreed that hearing voices in your head is not a good sign. To be fair, there *are* worse places to hear voices. Regardless, they're really going to help you in this round. Use your powers of deduction to analyse the tone, intonation and content of the following phrases to correctly identify the speaker. *Answers on page* 125.

A) 'Yo! Hut!'

☞ ________________________________

B) 'Thith ith therapth … He'th a thilly old thing.'

☞ ________________________________

C) 'Carrion regardless, as you might say.'

☞ ________________________________

D) 'Hah! No more closets and cellars for this bogey!'

☞ ________________________________

E) 'Woof bloody woof.'

☞ ________________________________

F) 'Never build a dungeon you wouldn't be happy to spend the night in yourself.'

☞ ________________________________

G) 'She went for a moonlight swim in what turned out to be a crocodile.'

☞ ________________________________

H) 'Anti-dragon cream. Personal guarantee; if you're incinerated you get your money back, no quibble.'

☞ ________________________________

I) 'Whoops, here comes Mr Jelly.'

☞ ________________________________

J) 'This vampiring's not all it's cracked up to be, you know. Can't go out in daylight, can't eat garlic, can't have a decent shave.'

☞ ________________________________

K) 'SOMETIMES PEOPLE CHALLENGE ME TO A GAME. FOR THEIR LIVES, YOU KNOW … LAST YEAR SOMEONE GOT THREE STREETS AND ALL THE UTILITIES.'

☞ ________________________________

L) 'Baths is unhygienic … You know I've never agreed with baths, sittin' around in your own dirt like that.'

☞ ________________________________

M) 'Luck is my middle name … Mind you, my first name is Bad.'

☞ ________________________________

N) 'Wotcher, Magrat. Pull up a chair and call the cat a bastard.'

☞ ________________________________

O) 'Bing bong bingely beep.'

☞ ________________________________

P) 'Dat's der bunny.'

☞ ________________________________

Q) 'Never say die, master. That's our motto, eh?'

☞ ________________________________

R) 'Bastards! That's because I was the one who woke up groaning in a pile of recycled chilli. Just once, I mean just once, I'd like to open my eyes in the morning without my head sticking to something.'

☞ ________________________________

S) 'Ah, right, sir. From now on I shall remember that you always said that, sir.'

☞ ________________________________

T) 'Not Watch business! ... Nothing to do with the Watch at all! We are just civilians, alright?'

☞ ________________________________

U) ' ... the finest tradition of the Watch is having a quiet smoke somewhere out of the wind at 3 a.m. Let's not get carried away, eh?'

☞ ________________________________

V) 'Never let me down, my lucky arrow didn't. Hit whatever I shot at. Hardly even had to aim. If that dragon's got any voonerables, that arrow'll find 'em.'

☞ ________________________________

W) 'Don't let me detain you.'

☞ ________________________________

X) 'There's no greys, only white that's got grubby.'

☞ ________________________________

Y) 'All the necklashes and shtuff. All the gold collarsh. They've got lotsh of them. Thatsh prieshts for you ... Nothing but torc, torc, torc ... '

☞ ________________________________

Z) 'Er. I don't know – I MEAN, I DON'T KNOW WHICH ONE HE IS.'

☞ ________________________________

AWARD YOURSELF ONE DISCWORLD TRIVIA POINT FOR EACH ORATOR CORRECTLY IDENTIFIED!

YOUR SCORE SO FAR: ________

- FOOD AND DRINK -

MONDAY 21ST OCT

169. Fred Colon is partial to a pint known as 'Winkles Old __'?

☞ ------------------------

TUESDAY 22ND OCT

WEDNESDAY 23RD OCT

170. Reannual plants, such as Vul Nut, are special in which particular way?

☞ ------------------------

THURSDAY 24TH OCT

ANSWERS

169. *Peculiar*

170. *They grow backwards in time. You sow the seed this year and they grow last year*

171. *Trolls* **172.** *Knurd*

FRIDAY 25TH OCT

SATURDAY 26TH OCT

SUNDAY 27TH OCT

171. Pitchblende Vindaloo is most appealing to which subset of Discworld denizens?

☞ ------------------------------

Diwali
Sto Plains Tiddly Winks Final

OCTEDA

YOUR BONUS FOR 3 POINTS!

172. Drinkers of the impossibly strong Klatchian Coffee soon learn that sobriety is simply the absence of drunkenness. What is the OPPOSITE of being drunk?

☞ ------------------------------

YOUR SCORE SO FAR: ______

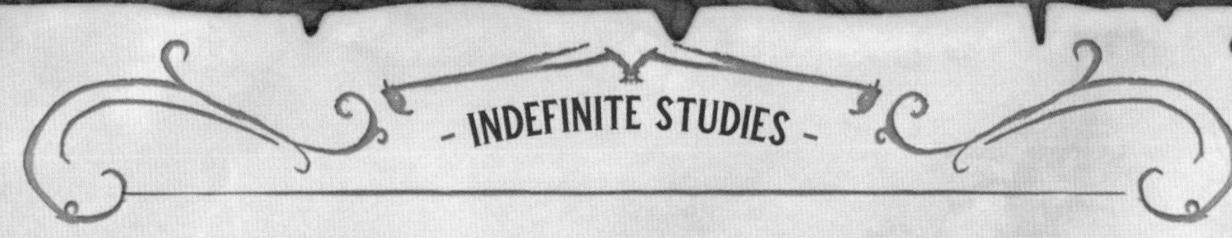

MONDAY 28TH OCT

173. Who is governess to Gawain and Twyla?

☞ ________________________

TUESDAY 29TH OCT

174. Who invented the 'spinning-up-into-the-air machine', the 'flapping-wing-flying-device' and the 'handy-note-scribbling-piece-of-paper-with-glue-that-comes-unstuck-when-you-want'?

☞ ____

WEDNESDAY 30TH OCT

THURSDAY 31ST OCT

ANSWERS

173. *Susan Sto Helit*
174. *Leonard of Quirm, he's a bit of a Detritus when it comes to thinking up names* **175.** *Ned Simnel*
176. *King Pteppicymon XXVIII – Pteppic/Teppic to his mates!*

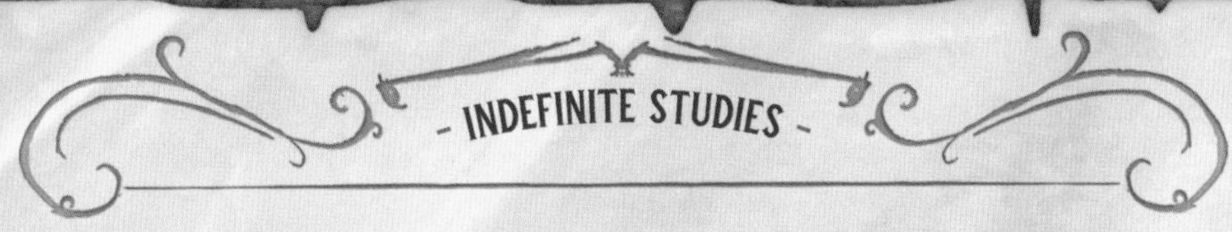

FRIDAY 1ST NOV

175. Who invented the Combination Harvester?

☞ ------------------------

SATURDAY 2ND NOV

SUNDAY 3RD NOV

OCTEDA…

YOUR BONUS FOR 3 POINTS!

176. Who is 'His Greatness the King, Lord of the Heavens, Charioteer of the Wagon of the Sun, Steersman of the Barque of the Sun, Guardian of the Secret Knowledge, Lord of the Horizon, Keeper of the Way, the Flail of Mercy, the High Born One, the Never Dying King'?

☞ ------------------------------------

YOUR SCORE SO FAR: ______

MONDAY 4TH NOV

TUESDAY 5TH NOV

177. Which of these is NOT a member of the Canting Crew: Tracy Morrow, Altogether Andrews, Coffin Henry or The Duck Man?

☞ --

Guy Fawkes' Night

WEDNESDAY 6TH NOV

THURSDAY 7TH NOV

178. In whose Ankh-Morpork cellar did thousands of 'snow globes' appear?

☞ --------------------------------

ANSWERS

177. *Tracy Morrow (who is, in fact, better known as American rap artist Ice-T)* **178.** *C.M.O.T. Dibbler* **179.** *Don't let me detain you* **180.** *He was assistant gardener at the palace*

FRIDAY 8TH NOV

179. What is Havelock Vetinari's favoured phrase for prematurely terminating a conversation?

☞ ---------------------------

SATURDAY 9TH NOV

SUNDAY 10TH NOV

Remembrance Sunday

OCTEDA

YOUR BONUS FOR 3 POINTS!

180. Where did Modo work before he became the gardener at Unseen University?

☞ ---------------------------

YOUR SCORE SO FAR: ______

MONDAY 11TH NOV

181. By which name are Draco Vulgaris also known?

☞ ____________________

Remembrance Day

TUESDAY 12TH NOV

WEDNESDAY 13TH NOV

THURSDAY 14TH NOV

182. According to Sir Terry in *Reaper Man*, what are the oldest living things on the Discworld?

☞ ____________________

Birthday of the Prince of Wales

ANSWERS

181. *Swamp Dragons!*
182. *Counting Pines*
183. *A Unicorn*
184. *Tharga Beasts*

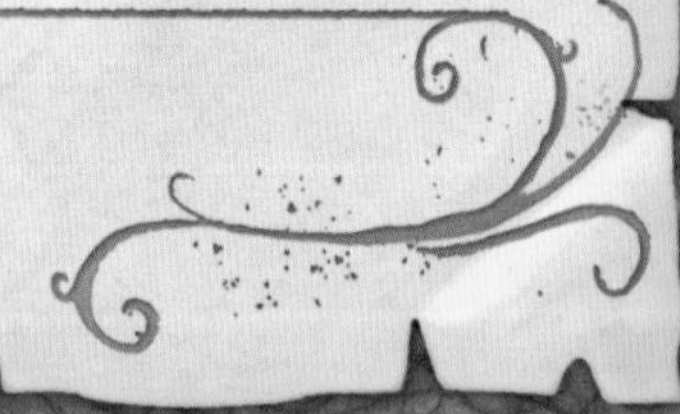

FRIDAY 15TH NOV

SATURDAY 16TH NOV

183. Which creature did Esme Weatherwax have Jason Ogg shoe with silver?

☞ ----------------------

SUNDAY 17TH NOV

OCTEDA

YOUR BONUS FOR 3 POINTS!

184. Which bovine beasts did Mort's family keep on the yard in their farm during the harsh winters?

☞ ----------------------------------

YOUR SCORE SO FAR: ______

MONDAY 18TH NOV

185. How many of her husbands has Nanny Ogg buried?

☞ ------------------

Start of Tattogey Week

TUESDAY 19TH NOV

WEDNESDAY 20TH NOV

186. Which witch turned a pumpkin into a royal coach and ended up in her own oven?

☞ ----------------------

THURSDAY 21ST NOV

ANSWERS

***185.** Three, at least two of which were already dead*

***186.** Black Aliss (Aliss Demurrage)* ***187.** Erzulie Gogol*

***188.** Nanny Annaple*

FRIDAY 22ND NOV

187. Which witch lives in a hut on four large duck feet?

☞ ------------------

SATURDAY 23RD NOV

SUNDAY 24TH NOV

OCTEDA

YOUR BONUS FOR 3 POINTS!

188. Which witch lost all her teeth by the time she was twenty and had a face like a sock full of marbles, making Esme jealous of her 'crone credibility'?

☞ ------------------------------

YOUR SCORE SO FAR: ______

MONDAY 25TH NOV

TUESDAY 26TH NOV

189. What do Mort and Ysabelle name their daughter?

☞ ------------------

WEDNESDAY 27TH NOV

THURSDAY 28TH NOV

190. What is the name of the uncle of Igor, son of Igor and Igorina, cousin to both Igor and Igor?

☞ ------------------------------

ANSWERS

189. *Susan Sto Helit*
190. *Igor*
191. *Seven! The eighth son of an eighth son has seven older brothers!*
192. *Nobby Nobbs*

FRIDAY 29TH NOV

SATURDAY 30TH NOV

St Andrew's Day (Scotland)

SUNDAY 1ST DEC

191. How many older brothers did Coin, the eponymous sourcerer in *Sourcery*, have?

☞ -------------------

First Sunday in Advent

OCTEDA...

YOUR BONUS FOR 3 POINTS!

192. Maisey and Sconner were the parents of which well-known character?

☞ ------------------------------------

YOUR SCORE SO FAR: ______

MONDAY 2ND DEC

193. Thunder rolled … but what did it roll?

☞ ______________________

TUESDAY 3RD DEC

WEDNESDAY 4TH DEC

194. Dragon King of Arms, chief Herald of Ankh-Morpork, belongs to which species?

☞ ______________________

THURSDAY 5TH DEC

ANSWERS

193. *It rolled a six. It is said that the gods play games with the lives of men, after all* **194.** *Vampire* **195.** *Octiron* **196.** *A Bogeyman, or more accurately THE Bogeyman. The very first*

FRIDAY 6TH DEC

195. Of which metal is the needle of a Discworldian compass made, to attract it to the high magical field of the Hub?

☞ ---------------------------------

SATURDAY 7TH DEC

SUNDAY 8TH DEC

OCTEDA

YOUR BONUS FOR 3 POINTS!

196. What species was the ORIGINAL tooth fairy who Susan meets in *Hogfather*?

☞ ---------------------------------

YOUR SCORE SO FAR: ______

- ODDEST ONE OUT -

There's always one who goes against the grain. The one who pushes the pull door, the giggler at the funeral, the eunuch at the orgy. This round is all about the odd one out.

We'd like to take the opportunity to underline the fact that we're an inclusive, equal opportunities quiz compiler and do not condone the singling out of 'individuals of difference', so in this round we'd like you to single them out instead! *Answers on page* 125.

A)
BLIND IO
BILIOUS
ANOIA
OFFLER

☞ ------------------

B)
ROUTER
SNOUTER
GOUGER
SNUFFLER

☞ ------------------

C)
IGOR
IGOR
IGOR
IGOR

☞ ------------------

D)
BOROGRAVIA
BONK
BES PELARGIC
AL-YBI

☞ ------------------

E)
SLIPNIR
ANKH
GREAT NEF
HUNG

☞ ------------------

F)
WAR
FAMINE
PESTILENCE
CHESTY

☞ ------------------

G)
STROON
BERILIA
TUBUL
GREAT T'PHON

☞ ------------------

H)
ALL JOLSON
COFFIN HENRY
ARNOLD SIDEWAYS
FOUL OLE RON

☞ ------------------

I)
TURBOT'S REALLY ODD
PEACH CORNICHE
LUGLARR
WINKLES OLD PECULIAR

☞ ------------------

J)

LANCE-CONSTABLE CUDDY

DECCAN RIBOBE

MISS FLITWORTH

MRS CAKE

☞ ------------------

K)

FIGGINS

DISTRESSED PUDDING

TITO

GENOCIDE BY CHOCOLATE

☞ ------------------

L)

THE DOME OF SKY

THE POOL OF NIGHT

THE IMPORTANCE OF WASHING HANDS

THE ARTICULATE RAVEN

☞ ------------------

M)

BRAVD THE HUBLANDER

BOY WILLIE

OLD VINCENT

MAD HAMISH

☞ ------------------

N)

RAMMEROCK

TROLLBONE

GORUNNA

CARRICK

☞ ------------------

O)

DRUM BILLET

WINDLE POONS

CUTANGLE

ZLORF FLANNELFOOT

☞ ------------------

P)

THE LIBRARIAN

QUOTH

GASPODE

ERIC'S PARROT

☞ ------------------

Q)

JOSIAH BOGGIS

ROSIE PALM

DR WHITEFACE

WEE MAD ARTHUR

☞ ------------------

R)

AGNES NITT

HUGHNON RIDCULLY

ADORA BELLE DEARHEART

EDWARD D'EATH

☞ ------------------

S)

MAUDLIN

CONTRACT

DEOSIL

PON'S

☞ ------------------

T)

RONALD SAVELOY

SUSAN STO HELIT

EULALIE BUTTS

VICTOR TUGELBEND

☞ ------------------

ONE DISCWORLD TRIVIA POINT FOR EACH ODD ONE OUT SPOTTED!

YOUR SCORE SO FAR: ______

MONDAY 9TH DEC

TUESDAY 10TH DEC

197. Minty Rocksmacker was once romantically linked to which prominent Watchman?

☞ ------------------------

WEDNESDAY 11TH DEC

THURSDAY 12TH DEC

198. When the Death of Rats is allowed to 'live on', during *Reaper Man*, which other 'lesser Death' is also spared?

☞ ------------------------------

ANSWERS

197. *Carrot Ironfoundersson, back in the Copperhead mines*

198. *The oft-forgotten Death of Fleas* **199.** *Snow... and a robin. IT WAS NOT AT ALL CO-OPERATIVE* **200.** *Snouter!*

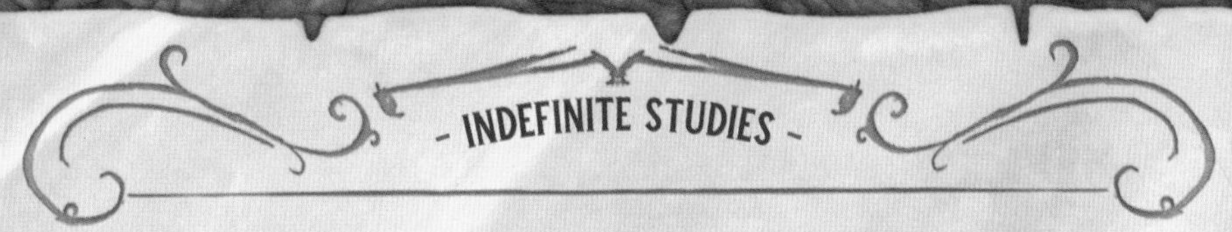

FRIDAY 13TH DEC

SATURDAY 14TH DEC

199. What did Death attempt to stick to his homemade Hogswach card to Susan?

☞ ----------------------

SUNDAY 15TH DEC

OCTEDA

YOUR BONUS FOR 3 POINTS!

200. The Hogfather's sleigh is pulled by Rooter, Gouger, Tusker and which other porcine puller?

☞ ----------------------------

YOUR SCORE SO FAR: ______

- 'TWAS THE NIGHT BEFORE HOGSWATCH -

MONDAY 16TH DEC

201. On Hogswatchnight, Archchancellor Ridcully offers to cure the Oh God of Hangovers with which condiment?

☞ ________________________________

TUESDAY 17TH DEC

WEDNESDAY 18TH DEC

202. Who takes out a contract with the Assassins' Guild for the Hogfather to be 'brought to an end'?

☞ ________________________________

THURSDAY 19TH DEC

ANSWERS

201. *Wow-wow sauce*
202. *The Auditors*
203. *Peachy, one of Teatime's associates*
204. *HUMANS NEED FANTASY TO BE HUMAN. TO BE THE PLACE WHERE THE FALLING ANGEL MEETS THE RISING APE*

FRIDAY 20TH DEC

203. Who was scared to death of the Scissor Man?

☞ ------------------------

SATURDAY 21ST DEC

SUNDAY 22ND DEC

Winter Solstice – Winter begins

OCTEDA...

YOUR BONUS FOR 3 POINTS!

204. Why do humans need fantasy?

☞ ------------------------

YOUR SCORE SO FAR: ______

MONDAY 23RD DEC

205. Where does the true Hogfather live?

☞ ----------------------

TUESDAY 24TH DEC

Christmas Eve

WEDNESDAY 25TH DEC

Christmas Day – Public Holiday UK

THURSDAY 26TH DEC

206. Which department store hosts Death's grotto debut as the Hogfather?

☞ ----------------------

Boxing Day – Public Holiday UK

ANSWERS

205 *The Castle of Bones*
206. *Crumley's* **207.** *Hex*
208. *If we know Discworld fans ... almost certainly 'no', but we'll leave it to your discretion*

FRIDAY 27TH DEC

SATURDAY 28TH DEC

SUNDAY 29TH DEC

207. Which 'machine' believes it is 'entitled' to write a letter to the Hogfather?

☞ ----------------------------

OCTEDA…

YOUR BONUS FOR 3 POINTS!

208. … AND HAVE YOU, DEAR QUIZZER, BEEN A GOOD BO … A GOOD DWA … A GOOD GNO … … A GOOD INDIVIDUAL?'

☞ ----------------------------

YOUR SCORE SO FAR: ______

MONDAY 30TH DEC

Hogswatcheve

TUESDAY 31ST DEC

New Year's Eve
Hogswatchnight

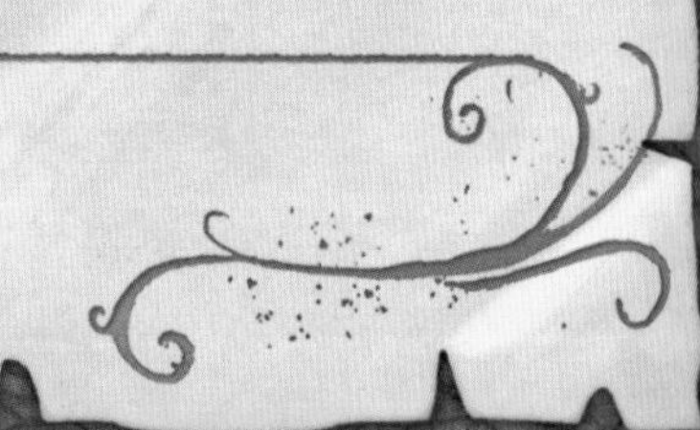

Congratulations on completing 2019 AND our quiz. When it comes to marking, we hope that you've kept an accurate and HONEST account of your performance, as we're about to begin the very exciting awards section! Sadly, our budget doesn't allow exciting sirens or flashy light shows. However, if you wish to purchase yourself a 'grand prize' we will endorse your decision whole-heartedly and attest herewith, to any partner, guardian, offspring or warden who tries to stand in your way, that their Figgins may be placed upon a spike and their forn parts torn asunder.

We've implemented a self-assessment system for our self-certification scheme, ensuring each and every quizzer, regardless of their performance, qualifies for a certificate.

Without further ado, measure your score on the chart overleaf and fill out your certificate so that you may be the -ing envy of all your friends.

CONGRATULATIONS CLASS OF 2019.

Answers

ANAGRAMS *(Pages 22-23)*

CHARACTERS: **A)** *Samuel Vimes* **B)** *Moist Von Lipwig* **C)** *Gytha Ogg* **D)** *Tiffany Aching* **E)** *Death of Rats*

PLACES: **F)** *Dunmanifestin* **G)** *The Chalk* **H)** *The Shades* **I)** *Tower of Art* **J)** *Pseudopolis*

BOOKS: **K)** *Feet of Clay* **L)** *Carpe Jugulum* **M)** *Where's My Cow?* **N)** *Unseen Academicals* **O)** *The Octavo*

SPECIES: **P)** *Bogeymen* **Q)** *Gargoyles* **R)** *Nac Mac Feegle* **S)** *Banshee* **T)** *Werewolves*

ORGANISATIONS: **U)** *Fresh Start Club* **V)** *Golem Trust* **W)** *The Smoking Gnu* **X)** *The Lancre Morris Men* **Y)** *Campaign for Equal Heights*

FILL IN THE -ING BLANKS
(Pages 40-41)

A) *Literature* **B)** *Pets* **C)** *Knob* **D)** *CATS (The capital letters are compulsory if you want a point!)* **E)** *Oook (We'll accept Ook if the intonation is correct!)* **F)** *God(-eat-)god* **G)** *Bookshop* **H)** *Mechanics* **I)** *What* **J)** *BJORN (again, capital letters are a must!)* **K)** *Immaterial* **L)** *Rectangular* **M)** *Time* **N)** *Rocks* **O)** *Centipede* **P)** *Man* **Q)** *Taxation* **R)** *Shoving* **S)** *Luters* **T)** *Chicken* **U)** *Policemen*

OPENING LINES *(Pages 58-59)*

A) *Colour of Magic* **B)** *Hogfather* **C)** *Reaper Man* **D)** *Interesting Times* **E)** *Maskerade* **F)** *Small Gods* **G)** *~~Faust~~ Eric* **H)** *The Light Fantastic* **I)** *Equal Rites* **J)** *Guards! Guards!* **K)** *Mort* **L)** *Moving Pictures* **M)** *Sourcery* **N)** *Wyrd Sisters* **O)** *Jingo* **P)** *Feet of Clay*

READING ORDER
(Pages 70-71)

1) *The Colour of Magic*
2) *The Light Fantastic*
3) *Equal Rites*
4) *Mort*
5) *Sourcery*
6) *Wyrd Sisters*
7) *Pyramids*
8) *Guards! Guards!*
9) *~~Faust~~ Eric*
10) *Moving Pictures*
11) *Reaper Man*
12) *Witches Abroad*
13) *Small Gods*
14) *Lords and Ladies*
15) *Men at Arms*
16) *Soul Music*
17) *Interesting Times*
18) *Maskerade*
19) *Feet of Clay*
20) *Hogfather*
21) *Jingo*
22) *The Last Continent*
23) *Carpe Jugulum*
24) *The Fifth Elephant*
25) *The Truth*
26) *Thief of Time*
27) *The Last Hero*
28) *The Amazing Maurice and his Educated Rodents*
29) *Night Watch*
30) *The Wee Free Men*
31) *Monstrous Regiment*
32) *A Hat Full of Sky*
33) *Going Postal*
34) *Thud!*
35) *Wintersmith*
36) *Making Money*
37) *Unseen Academicals*
38) *I Shall Wear Midnight*
39) *Snuff*
40) *Raising Steam*
41) *The Shepherd's Crown*

TRUE OR FALSE?
(Pages 86-87)

A) *False, why would you even think such a thing?*
B) *True, Doughnut Jimmy himself!*
C) *False* **D)** *False*
E) *False, it is of course Binky* **F)** *False*
G) *False* **H)** *True, among others!*
I) *True* **J)** *False* **K)** *True* **L)** *True*
M) *False* **N)** *True* **O)** *True* **P)** *False*
Q) *False* **R)** *False* **S)** *True* **T)** *False (it's in Fourecks)* **U)** *False* **V)** *False*
W) *True (Galder Weatherwax, a distant cousin of Esme)*
X) *False* **Y)** *True* **Z)** *True*

WHOSE LINE IS IT... EH?
(Pages 98-99)

A) *The Dean*
B) *Igor*
C) *Quoth, surveying a battlefield*
D) *Schleppel*
E) *Gaspode the Wonder Dog*
F) *The Patrician, Lord Havelock Vetinari*
G) *Teppic*
H) *Cut-Me-Own-Throat Dibbler*
I) *The Bursar*
J) *Arthur Winkings, Count Notfaroutoe*
K) *Death*
L) *Granny Weatherwax*
M) *Rincewind*
N) *Gytha Ogg*
O) *The imp in Vimes' Disorganizer*
P) *Detritus*
Q) *Albert*
R) *Bilious, the Oh God of Hangovers*
S) *Carrot Ironfoundersson*
T) *Fred Colon, during one of his plain clothes campaigns*
U) *Sam Vimes*
V) *Fred Colon, the master tactician*
W) *Lord Vetinari*
X) *Esme Weatherwax*
Y) *Cohen the Barbarian*
Z) *Susan Sto Helit – she inherited a lot from her grandfather*

ODDEST ONE OUT *(Pages 114-115)*

A) *All are gods except Bilious, who is an Oh God.*
B) *All are Hogfathers' hogs except Snuffler.*
C) *They're all brothers of Igor, except Igor.*
D) *All are towns/cities except Borogravia which is a country.*
E) *All are rivers, except Great Nef which is a desert.*
F) *All are horsemen of the Apocralypse, except Chesty who is one of the four horsemen of the Common Cold.*
G) *All are world-bearing elephants except Stroon, which is a straw with built-in spoon.*
H) *All are Canting Crew members, except All Jolson, the enormous A-M chef.*
I) *All are alcoholic human drinks, except Luglarr, a near-suicidal troll drink.*
J) *All died on the page, except Mrs. Cake who is sadly alive and well.*
K) *All are Discworld desserts, except Tito, which is a Discworld Desert.*
L) *All are Caroc Cards, except the Articulate Raven, which is not.*
M) *All are members of the Silver Horde except Bravd, who is more of a freelancer.*
N) *All are mountain ranges except Gorunna, which is a deep-sea trench.*
O) *All are wizards, except Zlorf Flannelfoot who was an assassin.*
P) *All are animals who can speak Morporkian, except the Librarian.*
Q) *All are heads of their guild, except Wee Mad Arthur who refuses to join the Ratcatchers' Guild.*
R) *All of their first names start with vowels, Except Hughnon... that was a mean one, sorry.*
S) *All are bridges in Ankh-Morpork, except Deosil which is a city gate.*
T) *All are/were members of the teaching profession, except Victor who only progressed as far as a student at UU.*

- AWARDS -

0 POINTS

The 'Did Not Resuscitate' Award – This score band, though technically possible, is highly unlikely unless you're… vitally challenged.

0-10 POINTS

The 'Get Your Money's Worth' Award – In all probability, you've purchased this diary in error, but we applaud your conviction in completing the quiz regardless.

11-70 POINTS

The 'What Duck?' Award – You did your best, we're not saying you should have, but you did. You are required to repeat the year, but not the quiz.

71-130 POINTS

The 'Fresh Off the Boat' Award – You're probably new to Discworld… For a very reasonable fee we could… er… show you around some of the… interesting bits.

131-190 POINTS

The 'Discworld Denizen' Award – You've likely spent some serious time in Discworld and it's beginning to show! Well done!

191-250 POINTS

The 'Full Native' Award – You quite possibly spend more time in Discworld than this world. We salute your dedication. Just remember to come up for air once in a while.

251-310 POINTS

The 'Bloody Good' Award – This is a real achievement. You've attained a very respectable level of competence in this quiz and you should consider including this award on your CV/gravestone.

311-370 POINTS

The 'Really Bloody Good' Award – You've expertly walked the fine line between true achievement and trying too hard. How many professional quizzers do you know with a social life? Well done.

371-430 POINTS

The 'Auditors' Award – Some people are a whizz at cocktail parties, others achieve astounding feats of physical prowess, others are able to resist such distractions and master daft quizzes about fantasy worlds. Congratulations!

431-487 POINTS

The 'No One Likes a Smart Arse' Award – You've aced the test, but at what cost?

488-1000 POINTS

You cheated.

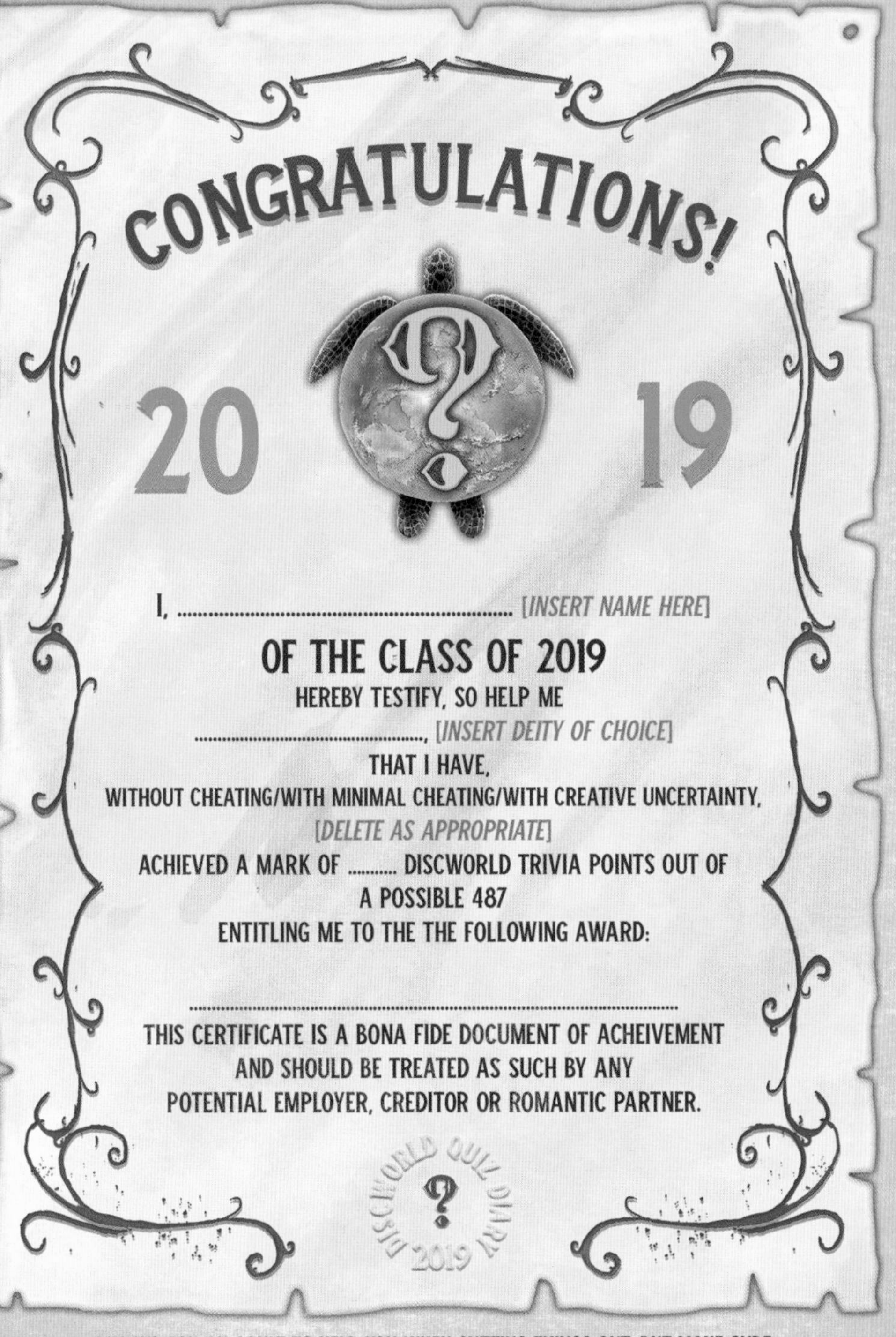

CONGRATULATIONS!

20 19

I, ... *[INSERT NAME HERE]*

OF THE CLASS OF 2019

HEREBY TESTIFY, SO HELP ME

...., *[INSERT DEITY OF CHOICE]*

THAT I HAVE,

WITHOUT CHEATING/WITH MINIMAL CHEATING/WITH CREATIVE UNCERTAINTY,

[DELETE AS APPROPRIATE]

ACHIEVED A MARK OF .... DISCWORLD TRIVIA POINTS OUT OF

A POSSIBLE 487

ENTITLING ME TO THE THE FOLLOWING AWARD:

....

THIS CERTIFICATE IS A BONA FIDE DOCUMENT OF ACHEIVEMENT

AND SHOULD BE TREATED AS SUCH BY ANY

POTENTIAL EMPLOYER, CREDITOR OR ROMANTIC PARTNER.

DISCWORLD QUIZ DIARY

2019

ALWAYS ASK AN ADULT TO HELP YOU WHEN CUTTING THINGS OUT, BUT MAKE SURE TO AGREE A PRICE WITH THEM FIRST!

- JANUARY -

S	M	T	W	T	F	S
			1	2	3	4
5	6	7	8	9	10	11
12	13	14	15	16	17	18
19	20	21	22	23	24	25
26	27	28	29	30	31	

- FEBRUARY -

S	M	T	W	T	F	S
						1
2	3	4	5	6	7	8
9	10	11	12	13	14	15
16	17	18	19	20	21	22
23	24	25	26	27	28	29

- MARCH -

S	M	T	W	T	F	S
1	2	3	4	5	6	7
8	9	10	11	12	13	14
15	16	17	18	19	20	21
22	23	24	25	26	27	28
29	30	31				

- APRIL -

S	M	T	W	T	F	S
			1	2	3	4
5	6	7	8	9	10	11
12	13	14	15	16	17	18
19	20	21	22	23	24	25
26	27	28	29	30		

- MAY -

S	M	T	W	T	F	S
					1	2
3	4	5	6	7	8	9
10	11	12	13	14	15	16
17	18	19	20	21	22	23
24	25	26	27	28	29	30
31						

- JUNE -

S	M	T	W	T	F	S
	1	2	3	4	5	6
7	8	9	10	11	12	13
14	15	16	17	18	19	20
21	22	23	24	25	26	27
28	29	30				

- 2020 -